NURSE MAGDA'S DILEMMA

Nurse Magda's Dilemma

by
Mary-Beth Williams

Dales Large Print Books
Long Preston, North Yorkshire,
England.

British Library Cataloguing in Publication Data.

Williams, Mary-Beth
   Nurse Magda's dilemma.

   A catalogue record for this book is
   available from the British Library

   ISBN 1-85389-777-9 pbk

First published in Great Britain by Robert Hale Ltd., 1979

Copyright © 1979 by Mary-Beth Williams

Cover illustration © Lesley Mackenzie by arrangement with
Allied Artists

The moral right of the author has been asserted

Published in Large Print 1997 by arrangement with Robert
Hale Ltd.

Dales Large Print is an imprint of
Library Magna Books Ltd.
Printed and bound in Great Britain by
T.J. International Ltd., Cornwall, PL28 8RW.

ONE

Magda Warren looked round the room which would be her own private retreat from now on, and liked it. It was bright and functional, with large windows and pale lavender-washed walls. The curtains and bedspread were matching cretonne, and pleasantly patterned with the most unlikely assortment of flowers ever to bloom at one time. So far the room looked a bit like one of many in a hotel, because she hadn't yet unpacked anything, not even a hair-brush, but she wanted to allow herself a few moments to ponder on the step she had taken, which was a very big one in any girl's life.

Magda was now a state-registered nurse, and—having taken the gold medal and the honour of being the best student in her year, in a West Country Hospital—she had decided against staying on as a staff-nurse at Huntingdales but had opted for a London Hospital and city experience. Her old Matron had quite understood, though regretfully, and, being a gold-medallist, Magda had found no difficulty in securing the first and only job for which she had applied at Darfield Park Hospital in South-east London.

There was no park, really, in the accepted sense, as she had discovered upon her interview a month ago. Darfield Park was a huge housing estate, and its tenants were the families of dock and factory workers and men from the giant gas-works nearby. After Huntingdales, Magda had never seen anything quite so awful. Even the few laurels struggling to grow in the area in front of the hospital looked tired and stunted. She looked from her window, now, across an area of tar-mac which separated the Nurses' Home from the hospital proper. The hospital had once been a workhouse, and looked it, though it had grown adjuncts of brick and concrete, which stuck up at each corner, making the shape of the hospital look, from the air, like the number five on a dice. The Nurses' Home rose seven storeys, and Magda's room was on the third floor. Up above were the probationer-nurses and on the first and second floors were the Sisters, with larger 'suites', containing their own bathrooms and minuscule kitchenettes.

Magda would have liked to stay on and become a Sister in due course, had it not been for the fact that she was engaged to be married. Moving to Darfield Park meant that she was nearer to Stanley—he would never allow her to call him Stan for short—and he was in practice in Bexington. The idea was that after about a year she would resign, marry Stanley and become his nurse-receptionist. Stanley had his surgery built on to a very nice red-brick house which had been his family home—his father had been a doctor, too—and it was all intended to be cosy and nice and what they both wanted.

As Stanley was leaving on a fishing holiday next day she decided she had better write him and post the letter in the box in the main hall of the hospital, to let him know she had safely arrived at Darfield Park. She could always unpack later.

'Dear Stanley,' (she began. They never were extravagant in their approaches to one another. Stanley was forty-three, had never had a serious girl friend before her and was reserved. This didn't mean he hadn't feelings. When they were together it was all said, and felt.) 'I've arrived at

9

this dark satanic mill of a place and am to see Matron—Sorry! The Senior Nursing Officer—tomorrow a.m. So I don't know where I'll be working, yet, but I'm keeping my fingers crossed it will be a surgical ward—'

A tap on her door made her jump. She didn't know anybody, yet, and presumed it was one of the maids.

'Come in!' she called.

A nurse wearing the jaunty cap of a staff-nurse at Darfield Park poked her red head round the door. With the red hair went the typical very blue eyes and freckles of one of such colouring.

'Hullo, I'm Briscoe,' announced the newcomer, giving her surname, first, as is usual in the nursing profession. 'Sister told us you had arrived. My name's Frances, but, Fran, please, to my friends.'

'Magda Warren.' She extended her hand readily. 'How nice of you to look me up!'

Another girl followed Fran Briscoe. She was dressed in mufti.

'Nights off,' she explained. 'I'm Dixon—Meg.' This girl was small, perfectly formed, almost a pocket-Venus, with dark hair and large brown eyes. She was a very lovely female indeed.

'I'm sorry I haven't a bottle of anything,' Magda apologised, shrugging at the room and her suitcases standing by the bed, 'but I haven't really moved in, yet.'

'That's O.K.,' Briscoe sat down on the bed. 'We were just off to the canteen for a cuppa and thought you'd like a bit of company on your first day. You can cut us dead any other time when you find your feet and make your own friends.'

'We trained together at Darfield Park and stayed on,' said Dixon, 'but what's your reason for coming here? It can't be the salubrious area. We're rather fond of the old joint but I can't imagine anyone in their right mind coming here out of choice.'

'I'm sure there are plenty of patients and I'm a nurse,' smiled Magda, not yet ready to confide. 'Is that an answer?'

'A dedicated answer,' decided Fran Briscoe. 'I think Meg rather hoped you were fleeing from a broken romance and were using Darfield Park as a hair-shirt, or something.'

'No, no broken romance,' Magda laughed. It was a long time since anything of the sort had been broken and she was surprised

11

at the thrill of remembered hurt in her laughter.

'Come on, then—' Fran threw open the door. 'The cup that cheers calls.'

'Do you mind if I—?' Magda held up a sheet of writing paper. 'I have to pop this in the box otherwise I may be reported as missing.'

'You can't miss the canteen by the row,' Fran explained, 'and our table will be surrounded by all Meg's followers.'

The shorter girl looked annoyed as the two disappeared and Magda shrugged. She supposed popularity could become boring with time. Still—she turned to the letter in her hands. '—I've just been visited by two very nice girls,' she wrote, 'and they want me to join them in the canteen so I'd better show willing. Look after yourself on Dartmoor and don't worry that Charles can't manage the practice. I'll see you my first long week-end.

Till then,
Magda.'

Again no impassioned phrases, no symbols for kisses. It could have been sister writing to brother. Yet all the happiness Magda had known for the past two and a half years had been in the company of

Doctor Stanley Orme, firstly in friendship on a holiday trip abroad, then in a deepening relationship that had been a long, long time coming to the kissing stage. By the time they were kissing they were engaged. Magda couldn't imagine Stanley asking a girl to go to bed with him, except as his wife. This made her feel safe and rather precious. She thought the old-fashioned standards had proved themselves; promiscuousness had scattered unhappiness like chaff in its wake.

She stamped the envelope and left her room, making for the main hall of the hospital and the post-box. She hoped Stanley enjoyed his lone fishing trip. He had gone fishing long before he had known her. Once she had accompanied him and fallen into a frozen sleep from which she awoke with cramp. Never again, she had vowed, but never was a long time.

She was standing in the raked quadrangle looking at the various direction boards when a male voice asked, 'Lost?'

'Not really.' A nice-looking young man smiled at her. 'I'm on my way to the canteen, actually, to join some friends.'

'So am I. My name's Trevelyan and you must be new here.'

'Yes. Magda Warren. Are you a doctor?'

'Guilty. This mad-house is the canteen. Who are your friends?'

'Nurses Briscoe and Dixon. I think I see them—'

'Yes. There they are. This way. Watch it, laddie!' as a houseman almost tipped his cup over Magda. 'Here's your lost lamb,' he announced, as though he was unaware of Meg Dixon's scarlet countenance and lowered eyes. 'Allow me to buy your tea and buns. How many are you? Six. Come on, Carter, help to carry.'

Magda was so aware of raw emotion in the air as she sat down trying not to look at Meg and at the same time being introduced to two young housemen. 'This is Ken Orrey, fancies himself no end and boasts of his conquests. Avoid him like the plague,' said Fran Briscoe in a loud voice, 'and Johnny, here, is rather a pet if you fancy the type, Eton and Oxford and thick as two short planks.'

'That's not very nice, Fran, when I took you to the Odeon only last week.'

'Only because you couldn't get Anderson or Dimlock to go with you. This is Harry Carter slopping the tea and Dr. Trevelyan, our kindly host on this occasion.'

14

The doctor moved away with a twinkle of his fingers and Meg asked suddenly and fiercely, 'Why had you to bring *him* along?'

Magda bit into an éclair before she answered.

'He kindly offered to show me the way and I thought him charming. Who is he? the devil in disguise?'

'Her boss on Alexandria Ward and the man she loves.'

'Oh, shut up, Fran!' flared Meg. 'You know he has a wife and three children.'

'So what difference—?' but Briscoe did shut up when she saw the gleam in her friend's eye.

'Where have you been all my life, my lovely?' asked the young Doctor Orrey, regarding Magda's dove-grey eyes and page-boy bobbed fair hair.

'Probably living my own,' she answered calmly.

'I'm sorry, Magda,' Meg suddenly said. 'We invite you for a cuppa and I fly at you like that. You must think we're a poor lot. Being on nights does get one down eventually.'

'How much longer have you to go?'

'Just over a week. Forgive me?' The

brown eyes were hurt and confused as they sought the grey. 'I am making a fool of myself, I know,' she whispered, 'but what's the cure?'

'I don't know. He does seem very nice. It almost seems wrong to say you'll get over it in time.'

'Don't get it wrong. He hasn't encouraged me in any way. I pray every night he will. There! It's out.'

Fran had sent the two young men for more cakes.

'I heard a rumour that Doctor Trevelyan's living-in. That he's left his wife. It's only a rumour, mind.'

Meg's countenance was a picture.

'Rumour's a strange growth in hospital,' Magda said quickly. 'At my last hospital one of our sisters went down with bronchial 'flu and rumour became rife that she was very ill with empyema and in no time at all we were collecting for a wreath. Of course she walked out of sick-bay while the collection was still going on and actually contributed. She was awfully amused by it all and interested in the amount collected. "No good giving it all back," she said. "Buy some flowers for the geriatrics with it," so we did, and threw in a potted plant

16

for her for being such a good sport.'

'Do you know which ward you'll be on?' Briscoe asked.

'No, not yet. I'm to see the Number One at nine-thirty tomorrow but I shouldn't think I'll start until Monday morning. When I came for interview I did say I preferred a surgical ward or theatre, but I had to agree to go where I was most needed so I may finish up on geriatrics. Poor old dears! They *have* to be nursed like anybody else.'

Magda was aware of Meg turning to watch Doctor Bill Trevelyan stride out of the canteen after drinking a cup of tea at the counter.

Ken Orrey addressed Magda.

'We must get together to really say hello,' he suggested. 'How about Wednesday at the George? I'll see you on the parking lot. I have a blue M.G.'

'Why wait five whole days?' asked Fran bluntly. 'Who are you saying hello to tomorrow, for instance?'

'You, Frances, are not my type. You mustn't be so jealous.'

'Jealous? me? Of you? Drop dead!'

'Wednesday *is* a while away,' Magda said, with a smile, 'and I can't make plans just yet. Thanks for asking me.'

'Oh, you I'll ask again,' came in honeyed tones.

'I'm going to unpack,' Magda decided. 'Thank you all for your company.'

There was a sour-smell outside carried by a sharp wind off the river; maybe there was a dye-works or sewage-farm fairly near.

'Why *did* I choose Darfield Park?' Magda now asked herself as she made her way back to the Nurses' Home. 'Because it was there, I suppose, like Everest.'

TWO

By the next morning Magda's room was looking more like home. She had put out the photographs of her parents against the background of her pleasant, detached home near Gloucester, and of her elder brother and his wife with their two-year-old son. Her silver-backed brushes, inherited from Great Aunt Catherine, gleamed on the dressing table and a couple of prints, a Renoir and a Manet hung from the picture rail. The wardrobe was full, now, and the drawers crammed with her new uniform dresses and undies.

She was in uniform this morning, for her visit to the Senior Nursing Officer, as was regulation now that she was officially on the staff. Senior members would look right through anybody wearing mufti, but recognise every face rising out of a uniform. One's individuality was somehow emphasized by the regimentation of the dress.

She went down when the breakfast bell rang and joined the throng in the main dining-hall, being urgently signalled by Nurse Briscoe to join her and six others at a long table. She was introduced to Gideon, a six-foot tall blonde, Prakesh, coffee-skinned and from India, originally, though her accent was Black Country; male-nurse Finglestein made himself known, both by himself as Daniel and Briscoe as 'Ikey-Mo'. It was all very good-natured and everybody tackled the lumpy porridge and the bacon and tomatoes with the gusto of the young, healthy and hungry.

'Boy friends?' asked Nurse Carrie Dale, frankly. 'Got any, Warren?'

19

'Well—'

'Of all the nosey-parkers!' Fran quickly came to the rescue. 'Just because you're newly-engaged to that garage-mechanic—'

'He's not just a mechanic, his father's the owner.'

'Well, then, be satisfied that you're so lucky. Most of us may plod these wards until we're pensioners. I must say Warren made an impression among the medical staff. Doctor Trevelyan escorted her to the canteen and Orrey actually offered her a foreseeable date at the George.'

'Lucky you!' said Nurse Gideon, who was rarely dated by tall, handsome men and refused to be seen in the company of those she termed 'dwarves', 'But watch out for him.'

'I promise,' smiled Magda, 'if I take up that invitation. I'm not desperate—yet.'

There was some laughter. There was always banter about the medical staff at any meal table.

Eventually the day staff made a concerted dash for the door and scattered to start their various duties. A few minutes later, while Magda was dallying over her third cup of coffee, the night-staff trailed in, some with hard, bright eyes and others who could barely keep their eyes open. Nurse Dixon came and flopped beside Magda.

'Hello! What a night! Two deaths and a diabetic coma. I only had three hours' sleep after leaving you. I would like to creep into bed instead of facing hospital fare, but the dining-room superintendent is such a hawk. She watches every mouthful. "Now, Nurse, we can't faint from hunger on duty, can we? We're here for the patients' sake. We need all our calories for them." What a life!'

'Deaths *are* depressing, especially at night,' Magda sympathised.

'Both were very ill. No, it's not the job. We're so desperately short-handed, though. My junior was pinched off me twice. As though we hadn't enough troubles of our own!'

'Do you find it easy to sleep during the day?'

'Now I do. I could sleep on a clothes-line. By the way, sorry if Briscoe and I made ourselves a pain in the neck to you yesterday. I was rather full of my self-inflicted wounds and Fran wears her size-nines and crashes them down regardless. Actually Doctor Orrey can be

21

quite pleasant. I mean he's good fun at parties, things like that, and a very good dancer.'

'I suppose I'll get to know him in due course.'

'You get all sorts in a hospital. Some one gets to know and others one doesn't, and the grass is always greener on the other side of the fence.'

'I don't think you should dwell on that,' said Magda.

Dixon's big brown eyes were watchful and wounded at the same time.

'I don't want to appear interfering,' Magda said quickly, 'but my impression when we were in that canteen, yesterday, was that you could have any man you wanted.'

'What a wrong impression!' Meg Dixon smiled wryly. 'But enough about that. I wonder where you'll be working?'

'I'll soon know. I feel my roll's slipping under my cap, if you'll excuse me I'll go and repair the damage. Mustn't look sloppy this morning, of all mornings.'

Already, she thought, as she redid her fair hair and pinned it up into a French-roll, which so well suited her when wearing a cap, she was becoming involved in this great hospital. She could not help thinking about Staff-nurse Dixon, so physically lovely and yet so obviously unhappy. Then there was Briscoe, who must know her friend like a familiar glove, and who also must have emotions and who, maybe, also loved someone. Magda had met both girls before in her other hospital; the beauty and the wit; the honeypot and the life and soul of the party.

She looked at herself critically in the mirror. She wouldn't call herself a raving beauty but her eyes were good, large and grey as doves' wings. Her nose was small, slightly tip-tilted. She had always admired girls with classical noses. She was five foot six and had been considered tall back at Huntingdales, but Nurse Briscoe could give her an inch and a half and she had positively to look up to Nurse Gideon. Her hair hung naturally in a page-boy bob, and she wore it loose except when in uniform. The rule that hair should be clear of the collar was not always rigidly adhered to nowadays, but Magda felt cleaner and fresher with her hair pinned up and out of the way.

She now gave herself a final over all

glance and approved what she saw. Darfield Park uniform was of bluebell blue and was overall style, lined for winter, and fastened all the way up the left hand side to the shoulder. Aprons were only worn if required. If one was doing a dressing-round, or humbler tasks like bed-panning and bottling, one took a sterile gown from the linen cupboard and donned it over the whole.

Her knees in the sheer black tights she wore shook a little as she approached the old workhouse building where the holy of holies was situated. Every small-paned window had an 'eyebrow' of jutting bricks, which gave the place a look of eternal inquiry. It must have been a cosy little hospital at one time when Darfield Park was perhaps a village, now it was probably only used as offices and stores and had an appearance of Victorian solidity hemmed in by the four connecting glass and concrete towers of its adjuncts.

KNOCK AND ENTER, she read as she reached the Senior Nursing Officer's room, and did so. At her interview she had been curious rather than nervous, investigating possibilities, only. But now she was 'of' Darfield Park she could be moved about like a pawn, and if she didn't like what she was asked to do there was little she could do about it. Her training had taught her early not to argue with those in authority.

The secretary, in her glassed-in cupboard, obligingly slid open the enquiry window and referred to her list.

'Nurse Warren? I have you down for nine-thirty. We're running a bit late. The Night-Superintendent had to have a lengthy discussion with Miss Toogood this morning. A bit of a flap last night, I believe, and the police were called. I should sit down and read a magazine over there.'

Magda looked for the first time 'over there' and saw another girl, also in Staff-Nurse's uniform, sitting on a bench seat and apparently reading Country Life.

'Hullo!' the magazine was lowered and a pair of short-sighted blue eyes blinked through heavy-rimmed spectacles. 'You new, too?'

'Yes. I didn't know there were two of us.'

'I only got in late last night and didn't go in to breakfast. I was a bit bilious—officially.'

25

'Oh,' said Magda.

'By the way, my name's Twine—Winnie.'

'I'm Magda Warren.'

The two shook hands.

'Actually I've come back again. I've already staffed for a year at Darfield Park. I left to get married and—and didn't. I should have been on my honeymoon instead of sitting here in a blue funk.'

'I—I'm sorry,' said Magda.

'Oh—it was mutual. No—' Nurse Twine was a poor liar— 'he didn't show up at the Register Office. He crawled back a couple of days ago and suggested we make it on another date but I—I had sort of been through hell and back again by then and told him nothing doing. Do you think I did right?'

Magda marvelled that complete strangers will tell their most intimate histories to outsiders. Maybe that way they sought an unbiased opinion.

'Without making that journey to hell and back again one really can't say,' she smiled ruefully.

'Which I hope you never have to,' said Nurse Twine. 'I must be a glutton for punishment. I even came back here where they all know about me.'

'Sisters under the skin,' Magda comforted. 'You must have made some friends.'

'Yes. Then there's work. That's the idea, to just work it off in familiar surroundings. I doubt I'll get my old ward back. My junior was all set to jump into my shoes. Matron won't want to demote her and I wouldn't want to work *under* her.'

'Which was your ward?'

'Children's medical. A gorgeous ward.'

A door opened and out floated a statuesque figure in a dark blue dress with a small white collar. Both nurses shot upright.

'Good morning, Sister,' said Twine, a greeting which Magda quickly echoed.

'Good morning, Nurses.' Actually the woman said 'Norses'. She looked again at Nurse Twine. 'Now where did you get yourself to? Had 'flu?' She went off without waiting for an answer.

'That's O'Rourke, the night-superintendent,' said Nurse Twine. 'Rumour has it that she, too, was left at the altar by a swine of a pathologist. There, eventually, go I,' she sighed, and jumped as a buzzer rang from the inner sanctum.

'That's me,' she said. 'Wish me luck.'

Though Magda did, wishes do not necessarily come true. Nurse Twine emerged from the S.N.O's office ten minutes later looking grim.

'Would you believe it?' she asked. 'I'm on Casualty. That's one hell of a department and Sister Casualty never relaxes for a second. I'm to go at once, they're short-staffed. Well, at least I won't have a minute to myself to fret or anything else. Be seeing you.'

The buzzer sounded again and the Secretary nodded in Magda's direction.

She tapped on the half-glassed door and was told to enter. She had already met Miss Toogood at her interview and found the lady charming and persuasive. On that occasion tea had appeared and they had enjoyed a chummy interlude, but now Miss Toogood looked harassed and did not even ask Magda to sit down.

'Ah! Nurse Warren. Welcome to Darfield Park!'

'Thank you.'

'I'm sorry to have to ask you to go on duty immediately. I know you're not officially supposed to start until Monday but you'll understand when I explain I now

28

have thirty-six nurses down with glandular fever.'

'I quite understand.'

A brief gleam of approval and then the pale eyes behind the spectacles roved over the desk again.

'I want you to staff in Victoria Ward, which is an acute medical ward. You will gain plenty of experience, there, which will stand you in good stead for the whole of your career.'

'But, Matron—'

Miss Toogood looked up suddenly, noting the agitated use of the old title and freezing a little.

'Yes, Nurse Warren?'

'I—I just wondered how long I can expect to be on Victoria Ward. I mean—am I just replacing a sick nurse for the duration?'

'You may expect to be there quite some time, Nurse. Staff Nurse Wagstaffe, whom you are replacing, has been laid low with one thing after another for months; she is very rundown and I shall have her watched closely. The health of my nurses is of great importance to me. Now I know you opted for a surgical appointment, but this is early in your state-registered career to take too hard a line about anything. What you need is experience. I suggest you go along immediately, Nurse, if that is all you wished to say. Report to Sister Golightly, and I hope you'll be very happy at Darfield Park.'

'I'm sure I shall.'

Magda brought her hands back to her sides, from where they had been clasped behind her back during this interview, and let herself out of the office. She asked the secretary the way to Victoria Ward and was surprised to be told it was in this old part of the building. Whereas the surgical wards were in modern blocks, as were the theatres and clinics and Out-patients, Victoria Ward was one of the old workhouse wards with beds facing each other down the length of the room, which seemed to disappear into infinity to Magda's eyes, used as they were to the lesser demand for beds in a West Country hospital. Its windows were high in the walls and the distemper on the walls a sickly shade of green. The washrooms and sluice were at the far end of the ward, as inconvenient as possible for the staff, who had to do a hundred yards' forbidden sprint every time the 'phone rang in the office. It is only fair to say that plans had been passed to build a modern medical block, but for two years there hadn't been the money in the civic purse to make a start on this project, and things were not improving on that score.

Magda, reporting to Sister Golightly, felt rather oppressed by her surroundings.

'Well, thank goodness they've sent us somebody,' Sister said rather busily. 'I haven't had a minute for the office. I'll take you round and introduce you to the other staff and then you're on your own. I have a Sisters' meeting at ten-thirty and then you're in charge for half an hour or so. Sure you can manage?'

Magda downed a wave of panic in a quick question.

'Have we any D.I.P's in at the moment, Sister?'

'Nobody's very well on an acute ward, Staff. We have some nasty chest cases in at the moment, four pneumonias and a pleurisy, also two renal failures. But I think they should all do until I get back.'

'Yes, Sister,' Magda accepted the professional reproof with a slight flush. 'I'm sure they will.'

She was introduced to the senior

probationer, one Nurse Murton, with a very plummy accent and who was nicknamed the 'deb'. The second year was a typical cockney, Everard, as bright and chirpy as the traditional London sparrows, and the first year was Dewhurst, a raw-boned girl from the West Riding of Yorkshire.

No sooner had names been exchanged than everybody flew back to the jobs in hand, the first year probationer to the sluice, the second and third years to the bed-making round and Magda on Sister's heels back to the office, asking what she was required to do.

'Well, hold the fort, of course, Staff. See the others go to coffee as they can be spared and you can have a cup of mine in the office, this once. I keep it in the cupboard and here are my keys. It's not an official rounds day but you never know who may decide to turn up, so see they all get a move on, that the place looks tidy and familiarize yourself with the patients. Here's the day-book and the night staff's report which I'll fill in later. Now I must positively fly.'

Magda stood to attention until Sister had gone, then took the book in her hands and entered the ward. Everybody looked as though they were asleep or dead, but she told herself an acute medical ward is not noted for indulging in high jinks and called to the junior nurse as she appeared from the sluice, her hands and arms red from scrubbing.

'Nurse—Dewhurst, is it? Go to coffee. Make it as quick as you can.'

'Right, Staff. 'ustle, bustle. Wagstaffe knew wot she were doin' goin' sick, an' no mistake.'

Magda consulted the day-book and approached the first bed on her left and smiled a resolute, encouraging smile at its occupant.

THREE

Mrs. Joyce Worthing lay in an oxygen tent, wan, but breathing quietly and regularly. She was the one who suffered from the effects of a rheumatic heart, and mostly managed to live with her disability, but had suddenly gone into acute heart-failure.

'How are you, Mrs. Worthing?' Magda mouthed through the transparent tent.

The woman opened her eyes and gave a little smile.

'Quite comfortable, thank you, Staff. I had a good night.'

Magda felt the first glow of satisfaction since entering Victoria Ward, and trust it to be a patient who made one feel like that.

So, in better heart, she greeted Miss Cantwell, yellow from the effects of jaundice, and Mrs. Dewar, now recovering from lobar pneumonia, and Mrs. Pretty, who wasn't, but was certainly talkative and wanted to tell Magda about all the other patients' symptoms in addition to her own.

Almost at the end of her getting-to-know-you round, Magda became aware of a white-coated figure at the entrance to the ward, foot-tapping in some impatience. She went smartly to meet the newcomer.

'Good morning, Doctor, I—'

'Good *afternoon*, you mean, Staff-nurse. I've been here awaiting your pleasure at least five minutes.'

Magda's first impressions were of a broad back as he turned to regard Mrs. Worthing. His hair was thick and leonine in colour and extended to his face. With horror Magda saw that one white sleeve was empty and tucked into the pocket of his white coat.

'Oh, Doctor, I—'

'Staff-nurse, what *are* we waiting for? May I have the patient's notes, please? *Do* get a move on!'

Pity changed to indignation in Magda's heart as she heard the irritation in the voice above her head. She banged her way back to the office, banged out again pulling the trolley containing the patients' files after her and re-entered the ward to find her visitor chatting quite amicably to the 'deb'.

'Coffee, Nurse,' Magda said quite sharply.

The bearded countenance was bent over Mrs. Worthing's folder as though it was an Agatha Christie thriller. Magda felt drawn to catch his eye, but he eluded her as he rammed the file back at her.

'Next,' he said, just as she was concluding they had met before. She rammed another file at him. Not only met, but loved and lost before. The broken glass splinters in her heart hurt as he threw the file back cheerfully, saying, 'Try again, Staff. I hope you're better at cards.'

For the whole round he never once glanced at her, though she would have recognised him anywhere, despite all that hair covering his face. She recognised the sand-coloured eyes teasing the patients, remembering how their gaze had once melted her limbs, and the strong, square, biting-teeth borrowed from some jungle predator. She remembered the lips drawing her soul from its very depths and then the playful little nip of the teeth at which she would protest, and laugh and regain her reason.

'Really, Staff-nurse, you are extremely dim today,' he chided her finally, and actually looked when she burst into tears and fled towards the office. He followed, dragging the discarded trolley, 'Now look here, Staff, if you're not well, say so. Maybe you, too, have this kissing disease that's rioting through the place even without the kissing, I may ruefully add. I suffered myself when I was but sixteen and never had the pleasure.'

She took her hankie from her eyes and regarded him.

'Good heavens!' he said. 'You're not Wagstaffe!'

'No.' She continued to look at him. 'Staff-nurse Wagstaffe is ill and I've been asked to take over.'

'Don't I know you?' he asked.

'Do you, Doctor Devon?'

'Take off your cap and let down your hair.'

'How can I? I'm on duty, and—'

But she might have known. He reached with his one good hand and she stood trembling before him, her hair curling under her ears and her eyes lowered, her colour high.

'By God! How long is it?'

'Three years.'

'What went wrong? Three years is a long time and I've been busy.'

'You asked me to marry you within the week and go away with you. I think it was to Malta.'

'Was that so bad, then?'

'I was in my first year and liked my job. I thought if you really loved me you'd let me finish my training and then come to you.'

'That sounds reasonable. I suppose being in love *is* a bit unreasonable. What a good thing we grow out of it. Did we have a row?'

'The daddy of all rows. It helped me to hate you as you walked away out of my life.'

'Good! Three years ago. I can scarcely believe it. Water under the bridge and all that. Do you think I could have a cup of coffee? Sister usually—'

'Oh, I'm sorry! She did say I could use her things.'

She took refuge in filling a kettle and plugging it in, spooning super-market coffee into two china mugs and being generous with the sugar.

'There!' she offered.

'Could you, I wonder, see to my arm, Mags?'

'Don't call me that!' she said sharply, happy that he had at least remembered her pet name. 'As you said, a lot of water has passed under the bridge.' She helped him out of his coat and jacket, happy to see he still had two arms, one of which was strapped to his chest.

'A fool called Orrey kicked me in a rugger-match and broke my clavicle. It'll be another two weeks before I can strangle the blighter.'

'Take care, Jon. He's my first date when I get some time off.'

'So you're not married or engaged or—or anything?'

'I don't think you have any right to—are

38

you engaged or married or—or anything?'

'Once engaged—no longer—plenty of everything.'

'Well, same here,' she said, thinking he hadn't allowed his heart to break over her, at least. Maybe women did put more importance on their love affairs.

She tightened the bandage over his arm which had grown a little slack and helped him back into his clothes. Even touching him sent remembered needles of awareness electrifyingly through her body, as though three years had not elapsed since she had been so completely physically in his power.

'I can't stop,' he now said, putting down the coffee mug. 'But we must get together, talk over old times. When're you free?'

'I don't know, yet. I've only been on duty a couple of hours.'

As she went back to the ward she began to realize what she had done three years ago. Love had walked out on her and it had hurt so much, she could neither eat nor sleep and her parents thought she was becoming anorexic. Then, hearing nothing more from Jon, not even a postcard, she had willed herself over the crisis and lost herself in her work. Meeting Stanley had been like sailing into a quiet harbour after drifting; here was affection, without passion, and safety. Stanley's kisses were benedictions, they did not demand. When she tried to give he would make a playful pass at her chin and say, 'After we're married, pet. After we're married. Don't play the temptress with an old hand like me.'

There he was somewhere on Dartmoor, playing his fish on his late summer holiday, and here was she with the one man who could make her heart turn a somersault likely to call in on her at any time, with his tawny eyes and great square biting teeth and the experiences of three years locked away in his bosom.

When Sister returned she was in quite a state.

'I'm sorry, Sister, but I'm not feeling at all myself. I really think you should ask for another Staff-nurse. I could be coming down with something.'

Sister knew sheer panic when she saw it, however.

'Right you are, Staff. I'll make an appointment for you with the Staff Physician in your lunch hour. It's better to be safe than sorry.'

But by lunchtime Magda had decided

problems are not solved by ducking them. If she saw enough of Jon Devon she would probably find out many of his less lovable characteristics; he hadn't exactly tried to impress her during the round; and by the time they had reminisced together and he had told her of his engagement, and she had confided about Stanley, then all would probably fall nicely into place and they could go on in their separate roles. It never did to look back and every fool knew there was no resuscitating old love; it went heavy and tasteless like yesterday's pudding.

★ ★ ★ ★

'Game to go for a Chinese meal on Monday, Warren?' Fran Briscoe asked that evening. 'We're all a bit sick of hospital stodge. At least at Ah Fong's everything's tasty if a bit ephemeral.'

'I'd love to come,' said Magda, who was hating her own company rather. She kept thinking of Stanley and feeling mean.

'Why?' she asked herself. 'I haven't done anything. I couldn't help meeting Jon again or feeling the way he makes me feel.'

'Talk to that twit of a friend of mine, would you?' Fan Briscoe persisted. 'She'll

41

be going on duty in half an hour and she's about to make a fool of herself.'

'Why should I have the power to stop her if you can't?'

'Because you're an observer who has seen some of the game, that's why. Stupid nurse falls in love with married doctor: married doctor apparently doesn't even notice stupid nurse for months on end, then suddenly asks her out. Do tackle her, Warren, or it'll be too late. That star-crossed Twine is making things worse, I do believe.'

Magda drifted over to the unlikely looking couple of the plain, bespectacled Winnie Twine and the lovely Meg Dixon, who was obviously blooming this evening.

'Hello!' Meg greeted happily. 'Did Fran send you over to talk me out of my date next Saturday?'

'Enough said,' Magda smiled. 'I won't breathe another word.'

'Single men are bad enough,' said Twine, 'but married men who ask single girls out are absolute sods.'

'When did one last ask you out?' Meg asked gaily.

'I wouldn't demean myself,' quoth Winnie. 'Go to the devil in your own

way, Dixon. It won't be a pretty sight.'
She went huffily away.

'I sometimes think nobody else knows
what being in love is,' Meg said rather
hopelessly, losing her mask of gaiety now
that half her audience was gone. 'Surely.
what I feel isn't unique? I feel impelled to
be with Bill.'

'I know how you feel,' Magda said.
'Have known,' she added. 'It doesn't make
sense for anybody else to advise you while
it's happening.'

'Ah! Somebody understands. Water in
the desert! Actually, I couldn't refuse. Not
the way he asked.'

'What do you mean "the way he
asked"?'

'Well, you know how I feel about him
but I didn't think he suspected, then he
asked me out of the blue if I liked children,
and I said yes, I loved them, and he asked
if I'd mind accompanying him on Saturday
to take two little kids on an outing. He said
I'd be doing him a favour. He's living in
hospital quarters so I suppose there's a rift
between him and his wife. But, of course,
he'll have access to his children. Well, what
would *you* have done?' she asked Magda.

'Probably agreed,' Magda decided, 'but

43

then, I'm not in love with the gentleman in question.'

'You think I'm taking a risk?'

'I don't know. You could be escalating a bad domestic situation, or you could get hurt. Only you can make your own decisions.'

'I've already decided. I've told him I'm going.'

'Talked some sense into her?' Fran's loud voice asked.

'Is that what you sent her to do?' Meg asked. 'Magda must think we're a real lot at Darfield Park, and no mistake. I'm going to supper. Goodnight, ladies.'

'Goodnight, Meg.'

Fran hurled her paper-backed novel across the room where it hit a knitter and caused her to drop a very important stitch.

★ ★ ★ ★

Sunday was supposedly a quiet day in hospital; there were no "rounds" and few domestics: a reduced nursing staff attempted to cope with more than was humanly possible, and usually managed by hook or by crook. Sisters were also inclined to have weekends off, and Sister

Golightly, having been done out of her normal weekend leave by a progression of events beyond her control, only turned up on Sunday morning to say she was not intending coming on duty.

'How will I manage, Sister?' Magda asked in desperation. 'It's only my second day.'

'Then you should be all the fresher to tackle it, Staff,' snapped Sister, sharply. 'I have been solidly on duty for nearly five weeks due to this damned epidemic we're having, and your dithering isn't going to stop me going to see my friend, who also happens to be a chiropodist.'

Sister limped off and Magda called, 'Sorry, Sister,' and began to help with the breakfasts. She hoped as she doled out porridge that there would be no emergencies, but her quick side-glances assured her that the more dangerously-ill patients seemed to be taking an interest in what was going on. Even Mrs. Worthing, sweating, was asking for the oxygen tent to be removed.

'Later, dear,' called Magda, indicating the procession of trolleys now blocking the aisle. 'I'll see to you myself.'

She was amazed when everything had

gone so smoothly that even a couple of bed baths were squeezed in before lunch, which was served on time. Oh, it wasn't going to be so bad on Victoria, she was suddenly convinced.

'You, Staff-nurse,' a white whirlwind stopped to address her. Oh! dear God, he was still capable of making her heart turn over just by appearing on the scene, like a genii out of a bottle.

'Yes, Doctor?' How cool and efficient she sounded!

'Get your skates on. There's an emergency coming up. Drug overdose with alcohol. Deep coma. Do what's necessary. O.K.?'

'O.K. Doctor. Very well, Doctor,' she quickly corrected herself, and metaphorically put her skates on.

FOUR

Magda had not expected to have so much responsibility thrust upon her young shoulders so early, but she had no time to fret about that fact for some time. There

46

was always an emergency bed kept vacant near the entrance to the ward, as Victoria had no side-wards, and this she now curtained off and rolled back the covers, while sending the ward junior for a couple of hot-water bottles.

'And tell Nurse Everard I would like a spare oxygen-cylinder, just in case.'

Jon Devon had gone off to act as escort to the patient, and when the trolley finally arrived, the patient covered by blue casualty blankets, it was accompanied by Staff-Nurse Twine.

'Oh, you again!' she said breezily. 'So we're both in the thick of it.'

'You girls can have a get together another time,' said Jon Devon, darkly. 'At the moment we're busy.'

'I need my blankets, please,' said Nurse Twine, and went off with a sympathetic grimace in Magda's direction, followed by the two porters and the trolley.

Magda could see that the patient, a slender, middle-aged woman, was in deep shock, and she pulled socks over the narrow, veined feet before tucking in the blankets. Jon Devon was busy with his stethoscope over the boney chest, he looked up to bark 'Oxygen!' and Magda

47

was able to say, hearing the racket outside, that it was coming.

Nurse Everard came hip first through the curtains dragging the cylinder with her, and said, excitedly, 'Cor! That's Divina Carlyon.'

'Friend of yours, Nurse?' asked Doctor Devon.

'Gosh! no. My mum was a fan of hers. She's the actress. My mum's got pictures of 'er in the family scrapbook. A bit past it, now. What's up with the old duck?'

'Nurse,' said Magda quietly, 'you're in charge of the ward while I'm in here. O.K.? Just go and carry on, and don't gossip. As soon as Nurse Murton returns I'd like to see her.'

Jon Devon observed, 'Asking Nurse Everard not to gossip is like asking Niagara to fall upwards. But you handled her very well. She grew two inches when you told her she was in charge.'

'We've all been young,' said Magda.

'Yes, Grandma,' he agreed. 'Face mask?'

'It's there, Doctor.'

'We'll give her some oxygen. I've injected coramine and there's a little bird gasping in there, but the heart sounds damaged, as though with an old rheumatic fever. I

48

don't want to do too much to her while she's hanging on but I want you to watch her like a hawk. I'll be in the office if you need me.'

'How long—?' her voice faded away in his frown.

'That's what one asks of the Lord, Staff-nurse. *I* don't happen to know. We're all probably more than ready for lunch.'

'I—!' she said, and then turned back to the patient. It was really quite hard at times to like Jon Devon, even though one had loved him. He had a nasty habit of reading one like a book.

She looked at the patient, and the oxygen-mask barely inflating. Drug over-dose with alcohol, he had said. Did that mean she had tried to take her life? How could anyone not want to live? Poor, poor soul!

The deb stirred the curtains. 'You wanted me, Staff?'

'Yes, Nurse. Could you manage the ward while the other two go to dinner?'

'Certainly. They're mostly all laid out napping, in any case.'

'Good! I would appreciate a cup of tea and a sandwich and Doctor's in the office. I suppose he, too, would—'

She saw the oxygen bag was lying suddenly limp, 'Hold on, Nurse, a moment! She's stopped breathing. Call Doctor Devon, would you?'

She ripped away the face mask, straddled the patient and thrust down her fists hard into the chest, 'Oh, no you don't!' she said, and took in a lungful of air before pressing her mouth to the other's. She had done this four times when Jon Devon took over and when it was replaced the oxygen bag reinflated more vigorously. They watched until there was a long, deep sigh from the patient and she turned her head slightly and opened pale-blue bleary eyes.

'You're fine, dear,' Magda assured her, quickly seeking one of the reaching hands. 'Go to sleep. We'll take care of you.'

Nurse Murton quietly deposited a tray.

'Oh, good! lunch,' said Jon Devon. 'How thoughtful of you, Nurse!'

'It was Staff's idea, sir.'

'Well, thank you, Staff.' He gave her an assessing glance. 'What happened to you, then, when you told me to go to hell and I did, on my own?'

Her heart began to thunder in her chest. 'Hell, sir? I thought you were bound for Malta.'

'Well, I never got there. You haven't answered my question.'

'I completed my training, as you can see.'

'I mean who was next? Who climbed up to that ivory tower and made you see sense? That some things are more important than a career, for instance?'

'*You* didn't think anything more important than your career.'

'A man has to have a job. But I wasn't thinking of my job when I drove my car over a quarry.'

'You had an accident? Oh, Jon!'

'I broke damn' near everything. That's why I never got to Malta. I was eighteen months in hospital and that's where I met Angela.'

'Angela?'

'Well, when you didn't answer my letter—'

'What letter?'

'You mean you didn't get my eight-page long letter written with my left hand?'

'I received no letter, Jon. You just walked off. Kaput!'

'Oh, look, we've got to meet and have a talk. I won't have any woman thinking I kiss and run without a backward glance.

I know a lot of time has passed but could you bear to hear my side of things?'

She wanted to ask 'About Angela?' but instead said, 'Of course we can talk.'

'I have a day off Tuesday.'

'I'm free at five.'

'Then meet me at the entrance to the Underground about 7 and we'll go up West and have a meal somewhere.'

'I'll look forward to that,' he said as he left.

The patient caught her eye with her own.

'Don't try to talk, dear,' said Magda. 'Just rest. You're going to be all right, you know.'

'I—I didn't mean to do what they'll all think,' the woman weakly protested. 'Please believe me, if nobody else does.'

'Of course.' Magda patted the thin hand. 'I believe it was all an accident and now we have to get you better. But you mustn't talk or I'll get shot. O.K.?' They exchanged a smile. Divina Carlyon? Magda wondered. The name was not totally unknown to her. Hadn't she once been a big name in a radio serial, which had now folded up? That was it. She had been in radio because of her lovely, deep, musical voice, but when the serial was in its hey-day Magda had been in her early teens. She remembered her mother always listening to the daily episode when she arrived home from school.

After another visit from Doctor Devon he pronounced the emergency's heart-beat much stronger.

'But she should be specialled for today,' he said, 'though *you* can't hang on here like a barnacle, you have other things to do, no doubt. Get that Lancashire lass in here. She's not as daft as she looks.'

'Quite apart from the fact that she comes from Yorkshire, Sir, I haven't found her daft at all.' Magda thought he deserved that, and sailed off to collect Nurse Dewhurst. 'Doctor will tell you what to look for, Nurse, and call me if there's any need.'

'Well, it's one way of taking your weight off your feet,' said the Yorkshire girl, which proved to Magda that she wasn't daft in any sense of the word.

Still, it was good to be able to stretch one's legs again, help with teas and have a word with the sicker of the patients, who had missed her these hours, or, rather, she preferred to think, the rank the uniform gave her.

'I say, Staff,' said Nurse Everard as they met in the kitchen, 'did she really try to do herself in?'

'Whatever are you talking about, Nurse?'

'Divina Carlyon. They say she took an overdose and there's a Bobby waiting outside the ward.'

'Nurse!' Magda frowned. 'I thought I asked you not to gossip?'

'I haven't said a dicky-bird, but I can't help putting two and two together. My mum would be upset if she went like that in the end.'

'Well, she isn't going,' Magda said firmly. 'We're seeing to it that she gets better. You're on your honour not to mention her outside the ward.'

'Cor! I have a day off tomorrow and my mum would—'

'Your mum won't hear a thing about Divina Carlyon from your lips, and that's an order. Now go and do the rubs and remember life must go on for us all as usual.'

★ ★ ★ ★

In the dining-room Nurse Twine was gesticulating frantically and Magda went over to join her. Briscoe was already there, as was Anne Gideon.

'Hear you've been having a bit of excitement on your ward,' said Fran. 'Twine's had bother keeping the Press at bay and even a T.V. camera-man's hanging about.'

Magda, fresh from playing escort while a W.P.C. talked to her newest patient and took down what seemed to be conclusive details that the woman had tried to take her life, sighed heavily.

'Look,' she said, 'I'm having enough trouble getting my own nurses not to talk about our domestic problems, without doing it myself. You know how it is. What's the lamb like?'

'Tough. And it's old mutton,' said Briscoe, chewing steadily. 'Of course it's marvellous for the teeth. I haven't needed a dentist since last Christmas.'

'Anyhow,' asked Anne Gideon, 'are you allowed to say how your apparently famous patient is?'

'Fine, now. Actually she has an old rheumatic-damaged heart and is likely to go into failure anytime. We have another one on the ward who—'

Her efforts to get the conversation away from Divina Carlyon were doomed to failure, however.

'When I saw her,' said Winnie Twine, 'I thought she was a goner. You got her round, then, Warren?'

'Doctor Devon did,' Magda spoke up. 'I only did as I was told.'

'Now there's a man after my own heart!' Briscoe put a hand to her chest. 'Dear, dear Jonathan! I could spit in Sister Fulham's eye every time I see her.'

'Sister Fulham?' Magda questioned.

'From minor theatres,' confided Gideon. 'About twenty-seven and a green-eyed blonde. Very attractive. I suppose it could be really on with those two and they have my blessing.'

'Mine, too,' added Fran generously. 'I take back my previous jealous remarks. She's nice and he's nice. The perfect ingredients of happy ever after.'

Magda felt a curious stabbing pain in her chest. How was it possible to have these reactions after so long. He had forgotten her in a romantic way, so why flog a dead horse? She had been eager to hear of his affair with Angela, and now his name was linked with a Sister from Minor Theatres.

'How's his arm?' Fran was asking, 'and if that grimace is indigestion I did warn you about the meat. Good for the teeth, terrible on the stomach.'

'Almost better, I think,' Magda replied, only wishing her trouble was indigestion. 'When he was doing the resuscitation I noticed he was using both arms, but he did put the bad one back in a sling later. I suppose he acted first and thought about that afterwards.'

'I had a letter from George today,' said Winnie Twine. 'He wants us to take up again where we left off.'

'Where was that, exactly?' Fran asked politely.

'I would tell him to take a long walk from a short pier,' said Anne Gideon.

'Ah, yes, but you haven't been in love, have you?'

'Go on, then, tell me what I've been missing. Don't forget all the juicy bits.'

'I think I'll say goodnight and get to bed,' said Magda, who didn't fancy the banter of the supper table any longer.

'Got a bad head?' asked Fran.

'Not really. But it has been a long, hard

day and I'm not really in harness, yet. See you all tomorrow, no doubt?'

'If not earlier, we're going to Ah Fong's. Remember?' Magda had forgotten but she smiled and said, 'At least I'll enjoy supper tomorrow, then.'

'I must pull myself together,' she decided as she brushed her hair into a shiny halo before the spotted mirror in her room. 'I can't run out on my friends like a wounded gazelle every time his name's mentioned, or fret that he's known other women in the meanwhile. Our affair, was three years ago and it's quite, quite over.'

FIVE

Magda arrived on duty and studied the case-histories of her patients, having been too busy to do so properly yesterday. She knew the questions relatives would ask, and as she was on duty until after the visiting hour she would have to answer all and sundry.

'When's my wife coming home, then, Nurse? The children miss her; I feel I can't cope with my job *and* them much longer.'

'Look, tell me frankly, is Mum going to get better or not?'

'What's dialysis, Nurse? My wife says you're waiting for dialysis before she'll feel any different.'

Finally, armed with Sister's small pocket day-book, which contained a potted history of each patient, Magda started on her own tour of the ward so that she could report on any deteriorations when Sister arrived—no doubt relieved by her visit to her chiropodist friend—half an hour later. She offered a gentle word of encouragement here, held a reaching hand for a moment there, weaving expertly in and out of breakfast trolleys which were in Nurse Murton's charge with Dewhurst providing her own comedy turn while instructing a nursing cadet, a young school-leaver who was trying the job out before actually committing herself to training two years hence.

'Nay, love,' came ringingly in Magda's wake. 'What's she want salt an' pepper for when she's on Bengers'? You must'a met a queer lot where yo've come from. Use your common. 'Ow can an intravenous feed be interested in bacon, egg an' tomato? You ever tried shoving that lot down a tube?'

'Good morning!' Magda finally greeted the newest patient, who opened heavy-lidded eyes which had been weeping. Funny enough nobody had thought to wash her and her mascara had run. 'Feeling better?'

'I'm very tired. Are you in charge here, Nurse?'

'At the moment until Sister arrives. I was on duty yesterday when you were brought to us.'

'And you thought I'd tried to commit suicide?'

'I don't know, Miss Carlyon. Our business was to revive you and I didn't think about much else at the time.'

'How did you know my name? That policewoman said I had no papers on me, and she made a point of the fact that I'd registered at the hotel under a false name using a non-existent address.'

'One of our nurses recognised you. Apparently her mother is a fan of yours.'

'Oh, Lord!' the other collapsed into her pillows. 'I didn't know there was anybody left who remembered *me*. The last role I played was as somebody's mother in a play, on stage, and I was only listed in very small print at the end of the programme. So the Police also have my name?'

'They had to be told whom we suspected you were, so I suppose they followed it up. Otherwise it makes it very difficult for everybody when a person is unknown. Especially—' she paused and bit her lip.

'Especially if they die, you mean?' Divina asked with a small smile. 'Don't worry, Nurse. I didn't want to die and you and that lovely young man saw to it that I damn' well didn't. I'm really grateful.'

'It's what we're here for. Now you should rest.'

'Well, when could I talk to you? I—I'm very worried.'

'Sister will want to see you. She wasn't on duty yesterday when you were admitted. Won't she do? Or perhaps, the Medical Social Worker if it's any sort of a problem the staff can't handle—?'

'I would rather like to talk to you, if you could manage five minutes. I remember opening my eyes and seeing you and you really looked as though you cared.'

Magda could hear noises in Sister's office and thought quickly.

'I'll come back later, Miss Carlyon, and

give you a wash and we'll put you into a nightie instead of that hospital gown. The hotel sent your case round so I have your things. Now I must buzz off and do my pill and potion round.' She gave a bright smile and vanished, hearing Nurse Dewhurst's hearty voice still in her wake.

'Come on, love. Whoops-a-daisy! Is that gorgeous son of yours coming visiting? The one 'oo looks like Robert Redford? He's not? Go on! That's really spoilt my day. Ah, well, life's more rocks than diamonds, as my Mum would say.'

The 'deb' said, 'Do hurry along, Nurse. Only half the beds made,' and then Sister was on the scene shooting six guns at once and handing out the mail at the same time. She called in the clinical room where Magda was loading up the medicine trolley against a list in her hand and said, 'Well, I apparently wasn't missed yesterday, after all. I must leave you to cope more often in future. What's this about an overdose in the emergency bed? Somebody out of Mrs. Dale's Diary, I do believe?'

'I don't think it was that one, Sister, but apparently she was quite a radio personality at one time. Also, this is only my opinion, I don't think she meant to take an overdose. She insists it was all an accident and I believe her.'

'The information I have is that she was found unconscious in a hotel bedroom where she had registered as Mrs. Jones, and gave a false address. So she was admitted here as an unknown person until Nurse Everard recognised her as the actress Divina Carlyon, which name was then filled in on her chart. Now if she was going off incognito to a rundown hotel like The Stag in Darfield Park, then exactly what conclusions would *you* draw, Staff? You saw her when she was admitted. Was she in need of resuscitation or not?'

'Yes, she was, Sister, but she does have a history of cardiac failure. I'm giving her a wash and changing her, when I've finished this, if that's all right with you, and I think I may learn more. She needs a friendly ear.'

'Hm. Well, do that, Staff, but remember this isn't a psychiatric unit and I want to know what goes on. She may think she's got round you with your pretty face, but I don't want to find her cutting her wrists on my ward or using my sheets as a garotte. If they mean it they'll do it somehow, I'm telling you.'

Eventually Magda drew the curtains round the actress's bed, filled a bowl and took Divina's toilet things from her bag. It struck her as odd that if someone intended taking their life they would have been so eager to pack soap, flannel and toothpaste and also an electric curling iron.

'I thought we'd freshen you up,' Magda said. 'I don't want to disturb you too much, so just leave it to me.'

'Am I allowed to talk?'

'Of course. But don't over-tire yourself, Miss Carlyon.'

'I'm Mrs. actually. Married and divorced. So my real name is Byngham. But that's history.'

'Would you rather we put you down as Byngham on your chart?'

'My God, no! I'll stick with old Divina whom most people, I assure you, have forgotten long ago. I hope all this is kept quiet. I suddenly woke in the night wondering what would happen if the papers found out, and they had to bring that nice young doctor to shut me up. He was awfully nice but I was vague about what had happened and I kept hearing somebody say "She tried to kill herself", which must have been the person who found me—the way I was. But I didn't and it was important to me to convince people. I'm not a ducker-out. I was very unhappy last night. Was it last night? Earlier? I've lost all conception of time. Am I boring you?'

'Not at all. Just close your eyes while I get the mascara off. There. I think you'll do. Now we'll put this nightie on. It's very pretty. Yellow suits you.'

'I was unhappy because of Eddie—'

'Look, Miss Carlyon, you don't have to tell me anything. I'm your nurse, not your confessor.'

'May I tell you? It would make me feel better.'

'Very well. I'll just do your hair. Shout if I pull.'

'I made Eddie my protégé; he was ambitious to get on the stage, into T.V., and I gave him the use of a room in my flat. In him I relived all my youthful ambitions, but there was never anything else—you know?—between us. At first he was like a son to me, more than anything, but as time went on, and he had some success, I did begin to feel warmer towards him, though I kept my feelings to myself, lacking encouragement. As he earned better

65

money he naturally wanted his own place, but I used every ruse to keep him with me. I pretended to be ill, and as I have a congenitally weak heart I could work myself up into throwing fainting fits. Well, it worked for a while; and then I think he grew suspicious and said he *had* to get away on his own, that we each had to go our own ways. Well, his way was up, in a T.V. series, and one of the jobs I'd been offered was as a peasant in a crowd in a new film. I had to dirty my face and cower from a horseman with a whip. I asked Eddie if there was a girl, and he said yes, there was, and rather than quarrel with him I asked him to bring her, but he told me rather nastily he didn't need my approval and to mind my own business. He wouldn't be back again, he said. After he'd gone I took a long look at myself in the mirror, forty-nine trying to look thirty, and not succeeding. I decided to go out and get drunk, and as we were known at most of the pubs round Blackheath I jumped on a 'bus and got off outside a place called "The Stag". I didn't even know the district. What is it?'

'Darfield Park, without the park. You've come slumming,' and Magda smiled.

'Well, I gave the first name that came

into my head and an address of some sort. After seeing a cockroach in my room I didn't intend staying more than one night, anyway. I sat at the bar and drank solidly, thinking it would make me sleepy, but I just became more and more sober and thought of Eddie with that girl, then about Debbie, my daughter—'

'You have a daughter?' Magda asked.

'Yes. I haven't seen her since she was twelve. Who would want to acknowledge a mother like me? She lives with her grandparents and Adrian, my husband, stays with them when he's in this country. He's mostly in Europe, though, with the E.E.C. But I was telling you—the drink didn't seem to do any good, so I took my sleeping pills as usual. I haven't slept well for years and always have some by me. I don't think I'd already taken some but I do recall taking two when I came out of the bathroom, but—as God is my judge—I didn't intentionally cheat. I had decided to accept an offer to go into rep and get on with my life without Eddie. When I woke up here my first thought was that the hotel had collapsed on me, I was so sore. My poor chest! Then the doctor told me how I'd had to be resuscitated and I realized what everybody must be thinking. Please believe me, Nurse, I *didn't* mean it. I wouldn't do a thing like that. Though I don't see Debbie, my daughter, I still wouldn't want her to have a mother who—'

'I do understand, Miss Carlyon.'

'And believe me?'

Magda was able to answer quite honestly.

'I do, yes. Now I think you should rest.'

'The doctor said the police would be coming back today, when I'm more settled. They're a different kettle of fish to you.'

'Just tell them the story you told me. They're usually very good and considerate. Now it's time for morning drinks and we're short-staffed, having a nurse off duty. I must go and get things organized. I want you to have a nice cup of Horlicks and get your strength back.'

'Just what I need to steady my nerves, Staff,' said Jon Devon, heading through the curtains and making her heart do its familiar flip-flop.

'Very well, sir, I'll see you get a cup, too,' she said as coolly as she could, because she had to make it quite clear that she had forgotten things, too, in their past.

Outside the kitchen she saw the young

doctor named Ken Orrey, casting a lascivious eye on the deb's distant ankles.

'Looking for someone, Doctor?' she asked.

'Oh, my sweet!' he followed her into the kitchen. 'Where have you been hiding? I thought you promised me a date?'

'I'm sure I didn't promise anything of the kind. I'm a very new girl here, and don't know when I'm free.'

'How about this evening?'

'Ah Fong's, with a group of girl friends.'

'You don't mean you're on a spinster's outing? *You?*'

'What's different about me?'

'Well, you're ' he drew a curvaceous silhouette with his hands and made to touch her cheek, but she ducked hurriedly.

'Tomorrow?' he asked. 'How about tomorrow?'

'She's going out tomorrow, too,' said Jon Devon, 'and why can't they find any work for you to do on Surgical? We're always very busy in our department.'

'Right, Sir,' Doctor Orrey said with just the right amount of deference to his impertinence. 'I'll go and find me some work to do and leave you to chat to the pretty lady.'

'That's my privilege as she's on one of my wards. We have patients to talk about.'

Magda felt a faint angry tingling in her blood as she was left watching a pan of milk while scooping Horlicks into mugs.

'Did you want to go out with him tomorrow?' Jon asked suddenly. 'I mean if you do, I'll willingly step down. It's just that I can't stand the lecherous little blighter, myself.'

'You are not a young woman, sir, though, are you? Gallantries are sometimes acceptable as an alternative to work. I admit it was not the time or place for such things, but I do like to do my own rejecting. I mean—I mean what right have you—?' She slammed a cup of Horlicks in his hand and went off with a tray into the ward.

'Sorry,' he said, behind her.

'That's all right.'

'You've gone all uppity, like a woman scorned.'

'Don't be ridiculous.'

'O.K. See you tomorrow.'

'I'll try to make it.' She knew when he had left. She felt the familiar ache of bereavement in her breast.

* ★ ★ ★ ★

Magda had a break at teatime but was back for the visiting hour on the ward. She saw Granny Benston's husband arrive with a bunch of dahlias and marigolds: he had a shiny pate edged with soft white fleece and a snowy beard. He could have doubled for Father Christmas any day. Soon everyone had a visitor apart from Divina Carlyon.

A young man came pushing into the office asking to see the actress.

'Are you family?' Magda asked.

'No. What's that got to do with it?'

His manner made Magda's hackles rise.

'Because Miss Carlyon, under strict doctor's orders, is not allowed visitors unless they are her family.'

'Does that mean she's kicking the bucket, then?'

'What charming phraseology! We rather hope not.'

'Then I'm going in. Try to stop me.'

'Having trouble?' asked Jon Devon, blocking the door adequately. He took his weak arm from its sling as though quite prepared to use it.

'He wants to see Miss Carlyon but he's

71

not a member of her family.'

'Oh well, that's it, then. Goodnight, chum! She'll send for you if she wants to see you.'

'You'll regret this,' said the fellow, whom Magda already thought of as the fly-by-night Eddie. 'Think you're a lot of little Hitlers, don't you?'

'You go off,' said Jon a moment later. 'I have some notes to write and I can do them right here. Ah Fong's, wasn't it? I can definitely recommend his sweet pancakes.'

SIX

Magda was only a quarter of an hour later than the others at Ah Fong's Chinese Restaurant.

'Good oh!' said Fran. 'Do you want an aperitif or can we start right in eating?'

'Let's eat,' Magda said, hearing the hungry note in her friend's voice. 'I'm starving.'

'We've settled for no. 5,' said Winnie Twine, 'that's spare-ribs, sweet and sour—'

'Anything,' Magda nodded.

She was introduced to Elsie Lyons, who was on Minor Theatres and Diana Freeman, a very pretty Jamaican girl.

'That's Sister Fulham over there on her own in the corner,' said Fran. 'She seems in a state, very upset and prone to tears. Elsie, here, thinks she ought to go over and ask what's up, but I don't know that's a good idea. I'm a great believer of the weep alone saying.'

'I suppose she is off duty and has a right to her personal feelings,' said Magda. 'I don't know Sister Golightly very well, yet, but I'm sure that if I caught her in a weak moment and dared to speak she'd be like a refrigerator.'

The spare-ribs were served by a youth whom Fran addressed as Who Flung Dung.

'They answer to anything,' she assured Magda, making puppy noises over the succulent food. 'You know why there are so many Chinese? It's because they can't bear to die and leave all this lovely food behind.'

Magda was glancing covertly at Sister Fulham. She had long dark-blonde hair done in a bun low on her neck. Her profile was classical and her lashes long. She was dwelling over a glass which she turned and turned in her long fingers. With a stab of jealousy Magda realized that she was a very lovely woman, the kind of Madonna who sometimes turns up among hospital sisters.

'I told George to buzz off when he 'phoned me,' Winnie Twine was saying, 'but I think I ought at least to keep him on a string. Make him dance a bit to *my* tune for a change.'

'Marry the poor blighter or let him go,' said Fran, darkly. 'It's so long since I had a date I might even take him on myself.'

'You're frustrated,' said Winnie. 'Anyway George hates red-heads.'

Fran choked on a bone.

'Well, man, if he don't like red-heads *I* can sure abandon any hope *I* might have had,' laughed the Jamaican in her calypso tones.

'Men aren't really necessary to our existence,' said Elsie Lyons. 'I don't mind admitting I've never had a boyfriend. I don't feel I've missed much.'

The various dishes were served on hot plates to Oohs and Aahs from the feasters, then a loud sibilant came from Fran's lips.

'Look who's just come in! I wonder if she was crying thinking he'd stood her up!'

Magda saw Jon Devon in earnest conversation with Sister Fulham. He was holding one of her hands and with the other took a playful swing at her chin, drawing a quavering smile in reply. Magda's heart hurt. She wanted to cry herself.

'Gosh! *I* think he's worth waiting for!' said Fran.

'Maybe he forgot the time,' Magda said quickly, 'or that he'd made a date. He told me to go early.'

'Nobody should forget a date with Sister Fulham,' said Elsie Lyons. 'I work with her and she's a sweetie.'

'Anyhow, she's cheered up, now,' Fran commentated, 'and they're ordering. Hello! What's this, Who Flung Dung?'

The laughing Chinese waiter was busily opening a bottle of Riesling.

'We didn't order wine, did we?' asked Winnie Twine worriedly. 'Gosh! So near the end of the month and I need new tights.'

'Compliments Doctor,' said the waiter.

Fran waved their acknowledgement over to the table in the corner.

'Thanks, sir!' she called out, and added quietly, 'Fancy him noticing us with *her* to look at.'

Magda had not even looked at the couple since the pain had seared her heart. Eating became a mechanical thing with her. She was worried about Stanley and the love she knew she couldn't offer him. Stanley wouldn't want to marry a woman who offered friendship only, even though he was fairly undemonstrative by nature. She had to think very seriously about Stanley.

'Are you engaged, Warren?' Elsie Lyons was asking.

It seemed everybody was hanging on her words and then she was saved by the bell. 'Well, ladies, how's the wine? Don't stint yourselves, there's another bottle to come.'

'Oh, Sir! Thank you, Sir!'

Magda couldn't speak, so conscious was she of the magnetic field between them.

'You know,' Fran considered, 'I have never known him to be particularly friendly to any of us girls off duty, before. In fact I would say he definitely is a keeper to himself. Not like Orrey and Carter, who think that buying you a beer is the first step to getting you into bed.'

'Briscoe!' objected Winnie Twine. 'That's really very coarse of you. A girl has to abide by her principles and any man knows exactly how far he can go with a girl if she makes it clear enough.'

'How far have *you* been?' Fran asked interestedly.

It seemed that soon they were on the pavement waiting for the 'bus back to the hospital. They would have walked but for the fact that temporarily they were replete and the wine had gone to their legs.

Magda would be glad to get to bed. Forcing herself not to be a skeleton at the feast had quite worn her out, and her last view of the couple in the corner had been of two heads so close together they could have kissed without effort, and probably would in the soft lighting of Ah Fong's, which Fran said was kept dull so that you strained your eyes reading the menu and thereafter couldn't see the prices.

★ ★ ★ ★

All hell seemed to be let loose next morning. Outpatients was crowded with strangers and Carruthers, the head porter, had donned an official looking uniform and was parading about saying 'Nah then! Nah then! Stop all this 'ere shovin'.'

Magda was greeted on the ward by an ambulant patient named Mrs. Tarby who waved a daily paper at her.

'Well, then! Look at that little lot, Nurse! We wondered why she was getting all that attention and now we know!'

She glared at Divina, who was sleeping, still, propped up on her pillows.

Magda read, DIVINA CARLYON IN SUICIDE BID HEROINE OF RADIO SERIAL THE LAWRENCE FAMILY TRIES TO END IT ALL.

Magda rammed the paper back at Mrs. Tarby and pushed Nurse Everard before her into the office.

'What's up, Staff?' asked that young lady. 'I'll never catch up before Sister comes.'

'You blabbed, didn't you?' Magda accused. 'You told your mother and she mentioned it to a friend and so it got to the papers.'

'I don't know what you're talking about. I—'

Sister swept in. 'I see we have a policeman guarding the ward. I never knew such a thing since I've been here. How did that happen?'

'Well, as you know, Sister, the Police accepted Miss Carlyon's story that it had been a mistake on her part, and were merely going to mention to the Press the bare facts in the kindest way. Nurse was off duty yesterday and must have told her mother, who was a fan of Miss Carlyon's, and so it spread with all the speculation changed into fact.'

Nurse Everard began to cry.

'Now, none of that, Nurse! Pull yourself together.'

'But I didn't breathe a word, Sister. I 'ad to bite my ruddy tongue but I would never go back on a promise an' I'd promised Staff.' She glared at Magda and sniffed.

'Very well, Nurse, we'll have to believe you. You may go and carry on with your work.'

'I'm sorry if I was over-hasty, Nurse,' Magda murmured.

'Well?' Jon Devon sailed in. 'Have you wallowed in the gutter press this morning? It seems our pretty young man really meant it when he said we'd be sorry, Staff-nurse. Good morning, Sister! Rotten for you.'

79

'What's this about a pretty young man?'

'He tried to gate-crash last night. When Staff told him only relatives were to be admitted to see Miss Carlyon he became most abusive and would have forced his way on to the ward had I not appeared. He went off muttering threats.'

'So he must have been the one who told the Press he had been living with Divina but that her demands had finally driven him away. He is to appear in a T.V. series and has plenty to say about that. He says he never loved her in the way she loved him but that he's sorry she tried to end her life in the way she did.'

There was a feeling of climax on the ward, and the one most affected slept through it all. Magda drew the curtains round the actress so that the other patients couldn't stare at her. Everybody expected the Press or the T.V. people to get through, and the policeman on duty certainly had to despatch some persistent characters, one of whom arrived saying he had come to repair a faulty cistern, but was found to have a camera in his bag of tools.

The staff were warned not to gossip with the patients, and the patients—especially those who were being a nuisance—told they would either be transferred to another ward or sent home as peace was essential on an acute medical ward. Gradually normality was restored and then nice things began to happen. Florists' vans rolled up in their scores and delivered bouquets, mostly from anonymous 'well-wishers', and some from friends, so that the ward was suddenly inundated. One offering, of pink roses, bore a card saying 'Darling Mummy, get well soon', and was signed 'Debbie'. Magda put that offering next to Divina, on her locker, together with the telegram from Brussels she was certain was from her husband. A large basket of fruits from the B.B.C. was placed in a corner together with a pile of written messages obviously handed in by people who—like Nurse Everard's mother—still remembered the actress in all her glory.

It was decided that when Divina awoke Doctor Devon was to be summoned to sedate her before he and Sister broke the news that the Press had got hold of her story and twisted it to suit their ends.

Apparently she took it all very philosophically, even asking to see the papers and smiling wryly over some versions. She called Magda in as she was passing.

'I'm sorry I brought all this on your dear hospital,' she apologised genuinely. 'I'm really surprised at Eddie. I let him go without a murmur at the finish and as to the "demands" I made upon him—! Will they believe—the public—that I only asked a little companionship now and again? I kept him, housed him and fed him and—when he was down—saw that he had the wherewithal to take a girl out to dinner. It seems he wants people to think we were lovers, but for what reason? How does he benefit from such a lie?'

'Maybe your career is a foundation stone he hopes to build on,' Magda decided, indicating the flowers and fruit and messages. 'You're not so unremembered as you imagined. There's a wardful of flowers out there, too. It looks like Kew Gardens.'

'And Debbie wants to see me,' Divina said softly, regarding the roses. 'I don't know if, after six years, I should wish it. Adrian has wired—so typical—that if I was in any difficulty I had only to let him know. He adds he may "look in". Honestly, Nurse, if I had the money I'd transfer myself to a Private Home and relieve you of all this.'

'No, don't go and leave us,' Magda said. 'I rather think Doctor Devon wants to look after you until you're better. He's aiming to be a cardiac specialist, you see, and you're grist to his mill. Now I won't be on duty at visiting time, so whom do you want to see?'

'I think if Debbie comes, I must see her, and then she'll see what an old hag I am. Adrian has a right to tell me off in person, so him, too. How many am I allowed?'

'Only two at once.'

'Well, I'd like to see Eddie if he comes—'

'He came last night. We had to send him away.'

'Oh, Nurse! I was—am—very fond of Eddie. Why did you do that?'

'Orders were that you were only allowed relatives. He was not very pleasant, I may add.'

'Oh, he can appear to have an unfortunate manner to some people. He can be quite, quite charming, however.'

'Very well, Miss Carlyon. I'll see he's not turned away again.'

An interviewer from the B.B.C. was

finally allowed to see Divina, with the news that their telephone lines had been flooded with calls after her welfare; also a reporter from an exclusive paper was granted the right to question. It looked as though all the sensationalism would die down, eventually, and the hospital run its normal course again. Meanwhile Magda's duty rota came to an end and she deliberately forgot what was happening on the ward, as a nurse must, and instead threw herself into preparations for the evening ahead of her. She washed her hair and curled it under, slightly, and then looked through her dresses. It had been gloomy, all day, and the nights were drawing in, so she decided on a bluebell-blue suit and navy, fairly high-heeled shoes. She didn't want to appear dressed to kill when she was apparently meeting another woman's fiancé just for a chat about old times: that those old times were assuming the importance of love's dream, for her, was just too bad when they were apparently water under the bridge for him.

Just before seven she arrived at Darfield Park station. Trains were pouring in from the city and discharging their loads, and one went off practically empty. She looked around but Jon wasn't there. Ten minutes later another train announced its arrival and about ten people who had collected in the meanwhile got in and the doors hissed shut. Magda had a moment of panic. He had forgotten or something was holding him up. She left the station and went back to look up and down the road. There he was, a mac over his arm, and he was—yes, he was running. This was the moment, three years ago, when she would have run to meet him, head back and eyes half closed and laughing mouth parted for a long, lingering kiss. She held her ground, however, and smiled cautiously.

'Hello!' she greeted.

'Hello you, too!' Without speaking his tawny eyes approved her appearance. He took her elbow and led her along the platform. 'Come on! Let's go and find a couple of good T-bone steaks.'

It was not a romantic statement but she thrilled to his touch, was almost glad when they sat opposite each other in the next train which happened along so there was no such electrifying contact possible.

SEVEN

The restaurant was small, sumptuous and underground: it was obviously a place the same clientéle favoured regularly. Jon was apparently well-known. A waiter showed Magda up by asking how his arm was. She had forgotten to do so.

'It really *is* O. K.?' she then asked, rather guiltily.

'Oh, yes. It'll do. Now were we going to talk about my life since Huntingdales, or yours?'

'Huntingdales has only just finished, for me, so it had better be yours. You put your car over a quarry and broke everything. That's as far as you got.'

'Yes, well, that was quite something for starters.

'Broken heart—' She stared at him for a moment but he continued— 'broken legs, a cracked vertebra, eight fingers—'

'You could have killed yourself,' she decided.

'And cared little,' he added, 'at the

86

time. It is not a bad exercise for a member of the medical profession to be at the business end of hypodermic needles for a change: to be helpless, to know pain quite intimately. Pain can be your whole world, cloud all your judgements. It is so demanding of one's attention there is nothing outside of it. That can be—in certain circumstances—a blessing in disguise.'

Not quite knowing what he meant she said, 'I can imagine it must have been horrible for you. You had always been so fit.'

'I wouldn't agree the word was horrible, exactly. Accidents happen every day. It's being a statistic and an observer of your own afflictions that creates a kind of morbid interest. I found I was testing myself for endurance; having been told to shout out when everything became too much I would tell myself, "Not yet. You can hang on a while, yet." It was as though I was enjoying wrestling with pain and winning, if only for a short time. But I am not here to give you a blow by blow account of my hospital days, except as they affect emotional experiences in these intervening years.'

'Her name was Angela,' Magda prompted with a smile which was more like a rictus bending her lips. 'You told me that much.'

'Ah, yes. So aptly named I thought when I first met her. She was a physiotherapist at the hospital. Now I know male patients are supposed to fall in love with their nurses, but I perversely hated all mine. They had me at their mercy, they could hurt me by just attending to me, and when I gave them the benefit of my not inconsiderable vocabulary of vituperation I used to imagine they did it on purpose, which was, of course, untrue and unkind. Perhaps I didn't have a nurse who was my ideal of a nurse, as you were.' Magda's brows shot up and down again. 'I had efficient girls and women who told me to come along, now, and not to be a naughty boy. Then one day I looked up and there she was, ash-blonde hair which bobbed into curls at the ends and emerald-green caring eyes. She was pressing into my chest, teaching me how to breathe properly with my strapped ribs. I took everything from her. When I hurt I laughed and let her hurt me again. She spent hours on me, and each visit I knew I loved her a little more. Once I asked her if she minded patients loving her. Not at all, she said, love helped a great deal in the healing process. Did she love me? Of course, she assured me. I told her we'd have a cottage at first, when we got married. We progressed and my ribs were unstrapped. I even lost my wretched corset. My fingers proved the most reluctant to heal—a damned good job I wasn't a surgeon—and Angela set me tasks to perform with modelling clay. I hated these sessions, as she used to leave me to it. I was more or less mobile with one leg in a caliper and could move around quite nimbly on crutches. It was obvious that I would live and work, providing the end—literally the ends—' he waved his fingers at her— 'recovered sufficiently for me to do what was required of them. One day she visited me and was quite cross because I hadn't finished making a plasticene elephant for her. I told her, somewhat sulkily, that I was rather a big boy for making baby elephants and she shouted at me for the first time. She said it wasn't the elephant, it was the manipulation of my fingers in creating the thing which counted. I could make

89

an aeroplane or a tractor if my masculinity was offended by her request, but I had better get busy or else—! I noticed as she went off that she was a big woman, at least five foot ten, and had muscular calves. I sulked and then I decided she should have the best plasticene elephant she had ever seen. I put my heart and soul and stiff fingers into creating a baby jumbo down to tiny tusks and toe nails. I made an orange howdah for good measure and went off to find my Angela. She wasn't on the ward. She was in the private block and I was directed to a small side-ward. It was one of those which has a window in the wall for observation of the very sick as well as having a half-glazed door. I looked in from the side and I saw those caring green eyes looking down at a youth who was strung up in a cradle over the bed. She was pressing on his chest and I could imagine her saying, encouragingly, "Now breathe in. Slowly. Out again. Did that hurt? Never mind. Try again—for me."

I waited till she came out and gave her the elephant.

'Mission accomplished,' I said. She gave me a funny look, half shy of me now that I was standing alongside her.

'Very good,' she said.

'Is *he* in love with you?' I asked, nodding at the sideward.

'I think so. But it's all quite temporary. They all get over it in time.'

She began to walk away.

'Are we ever going to get married?' I called after her.

She turned and gave me a very old fashioned look and studied the elephant in her hand.

'I shouldn't think so,' she said, 'and neither should you. Not now.'

'No. O.K.,' I said, and never realized I would feel quite so good about it. I was looking forward to getting back to work and a wife and all the shenanigans entailed might have complicated things a bit. So that's the way it was. It didn't hurt nearly so much the second time.'

'But people can and do fall in love again,' Magda insisted. 'Not many of my acquaintances married their first sweethearts.'

'I suppose it does depend on the first love,' said Jon, his tawny eyes apparently intent on his dessert. He then gazed upon her fully so that her very soul seemed to cringe within her under the impact. 'I had another experience after that one,' he told her, 'where the roles were entirely reversed. I fell in love with a patient; Angela's kind of love. I knew she was going to die from the beginning of it all and I like to think it helped that I could sit with her behind drawn curtains and create a mythical future for us while we held hands. I have asked myself, often, was it immoral? Pity, they say, is akin to love. When she did die it was not for the pity of it I cried.'

Magda found herself seizing his hand, patting it.

'Oh, Jon, you have so much love to give. It has to spill over. Now I hope that having got these two phoney experiences out of your system all will go well with you in future.'

'So do I. I haven't the instincts of a monk. Neither can I perform the one-night stand capers of the junior housemen. I feel like an older generation'

'Oh, Jon, you're twenty-nine. Come on!'

'Thirty next month,' he nodded.

'And there's hope for you, isn't there? In that direction, I mean?'

She didn't want to repeat the gossip from Ah Fong's.

'There *could* be hope. I'm playing it very much by ear at the moment. Once bitten twice shy, you know.'

'You're a very attractive man and I don't think you should belittle your chances with the opposite sex.'

'Your encouragement cheers me to hope anew. Now, what happened to you?'

Her grey eyes were suddenly large with alarm.

'Jon! Is that the time? I didn't ask for a late pass and I have to be in by eleven.'

He was suddenly all arms, paying, tipping, dragging her up the steps to the open air and heading for the nearest underground 'With luck you'll only be ten minutes late,' he decided.

At eleven-fifteen she was, indeed, outside the Nurses' Home. A chestnut tree waved its thin branches over them.

'Well,' gasped Jon, after running with her, 'Go on in and face the music—' she hesitated— 'or pay a forfeit.'

All in a moment her face was cradled in his hands and his lips had descended. More than three years might not have elapsed for her, it was the same old magic, the same drawing of the very life from her body.

'Oh, Jon!' she said weakly.

'I know. I'm making you more late. Off you go.'

She passed into the lighted hallway where Home-Sister said, half waggishly, 'Now *you're* not starting overstaying your leave, are you, Nurse Warren? I know, I know, you missed the 'bus. Off you go. Don't do it again.'

Fran was unaccountably at her elbow climbing the stairs as no lifts were allowed after half-past-ten.

'Was that you necking under that tree?'

'Oh, Fran, I'm tired.'

'Well, I don't mean to be nosey, but how do you do it? You haven't been here a week, yet.'

'I met an old friend and I wouldn't call it necking.'

'All right, so I'll shut up and mind my own business. I only know if I could manage one date which ended up with kisses I wouldn't be such an old misery-boots.'

Magda gave a grimace which was meant to be an apologetic smile and thankfully unlocked her room door. Here, in sanctuary, she sat on the bed and came to a decision. Jon's kiss had only underlined what she had known she must do for some time. She must tell Stanley she couldn't go on. Longingly she glanced at her watch, but it was now twenty-five past eleven and Stanley would be tucked up in bed after his day's fishing. He was an early riser, though, so she must get up early enough to catch him. There was no hope in her for the future but living a lie was totally unacceptable. Stanley would want to know if she was on the horns of a dilemma.

So, promptly at seven, she heard his voice from his lodgings on Dartmoor. He stayed with the same family every year.

'Magda? Is anything wrong?'

'I wouldn't say wrong, Stanley. I want to see you, that's all.'

'But I'll be back next week and you can see all you want of me, you silly girl.'

'Stanley, I don't want to wait 'till next week. I want to see you now.'

'You mean today?'

'Is it possible?'

'I suppose so if I got the ten a.m. from Exeter.'

'That would be fine. I have an afternoon so I'll meet your train. Thanks a lot. I have to go in to breakfast, now.'

'Fortunately I've had mine,' and he hung up.

She went into the dining hall in a daze, hauled to the table where her friends were like a rag doll.

'*You'd* better brighten up, Magda,' warned Fran Briscoe. 'Your big boss is back today, refreshed from holidaying in the Algarve.'

'My big boss?' Magda asked. 'Oh! the consultant,' she decided. 'Sir Vivian somebody or other.'

'Sir Vivian Rydale is not somebody-or-other,' said Anne Gideon. 'He's a V.I.P. hereabouts. You haven't met him, then?'

'No.' Magda was happy to talk about anything rather than think of her meeting with Stanley. 'Is he so awful, then?'

'Terrible,' Anne said, winking at Fran. 'He's the sort who'll have your guts for garters as soon as look at you. You'd better have your ward so spick and span that the Queen-Mother couldn't complain.'

'I was under Sir Vivian for a bit,' quoth Winnie Twine, 'when I first met George. He'd have enjoyed our Chinese meal the other night, he can use chopsticks.'

'Bully for Sir Vivian,' said Fran.

'Stupid! I meant George.'

96

'Sorry! But it's no good living in the past, Twine. We get George breakfast, dinner, tea and supper. Shut up about him, eh? or else run off and marry the poor blighter or somebody else.'

'You know what they say about girls who wear glasses,' blinked the other. 'I know I'm no beauty but, then, George isn't exactly Casanova, either. But we suited each other. At least, we did until he did that to me. I don't think there'll ever be another great love in *my* life.'

There followed a discussion as to whether love was possible more than once in a life time.

'Gosh! I hope so,' said Carrie Dale. 'I've been engaged twice and I certainly can't see myself ending up as an old maid.'

'Then you were never in love,' asserted Twine. 'It was merely sexual attraction. That can happen over and over.'

'Don't tell me about my own feelings,' Carrie said warmly. 'I loved Derek and I loved Tim. Only it didn't last.'

'Sex,' Winnie insisted.

'A fat lot *you* know about it. Anybody would think you're unique in having an affair of such immortal splendour as that of Lord Nelson and Lady Hamilton.'

'I think it's got to be able to happen more than once,' Fran said pacifically. 'What do you think, Magda?'

'Oh, I'm not exactly an authority.'

'You've never been in love?'

'I've felt deeply about somebody, yes. I don't think we should spurn sexual attraction. It has to be there for a relationship to function. Though not welcoming the idea I think one must be able to get over an affair and be given another chance. While one is involved one can't really believe it, but so many people do get over disappointments and tragedies to become happy again with someone else. I don't think they're all settling for second-best.' She felt a twinge of shame knowing she had been prepared to do just that with Stanley.

'I shall never love again,' said Winnie Twine, dramatically.

'That's your privilege,' snorted Carrie Moore, 'and quite a let off for all mankind.'

Before heated words could be exchanged Sister dining-room was breaking up the party and asking if nobody had any work to do that day.

EIGHT

It was amazing how Victoria Ward was ever ready to receive the presence of its Consulting Physician, Sir Vivian Rydale, and his retinue, but somehow most things were accomplished in time and Magda glanced round daring a speck of dust to show itself or a cobweb as a thin gleam of autumnal sunlight shone into a corner. At the last moment a patient on intake and output asked for a bed-pan. Magda smothered her irritation.

'Draw the curtains and see to her, Nurse,' she told Everard. 'Fortunately she's well down the ward. Don't forget to weigh and record. You get into the sluice, Nurse Dewhurst, and try not to be noisy.'

A moment later a procession came through the swing-doors. It was headed by a very tall, thin man with a generous thatch of rather tousled, silver hair. This individual wore an eye patch, but the visible remaining eye, sharply blue, took in the scene in one comprehensive darting glance. He walked with a forward, loping gait, and Magda immediately saw Sir Vivian as a cross between a pirate and the Pied Piper of Hamelin's fame.

'Good morning, Staff-nurse!' he greeted, without apparently having looked at her.

'Good morning, sir.' Magda was soon to know that Sir Vivian's one good eye never missed a thing.

'You're new,' he told the ward. 'Do you like us? Are we to your satisfaction?'

Assuming that he expected a reply Magda said quietly, 'I like working here very much, sir.'

'Good! Team spiwit. That's what I like in my wards. Team spiwit.'

Now Magda knew that her friends had been ragging her about Sir Vivian. Not only was he larger than life in appearance, but he couldn't pronounce his 'r's'.

Behind the consultant stood Jon Devon, at the ready, followed by Sister pulling a trolley bearing the patients' files. She indicated that her Staff-nurse take the trolley without more ado and Magda prayed silently that she knew all the patients sufficiently well, by now, to hand over the right file at the right time. Two medical housemen came next, Doctors Vincent and Patel, the latter a female with a sari under her white coat, and then Sir Vivian's medical secretary with her note-book and ballpoint at the ready, a girl physiotherapist and several students seeking a little practical experience, from a nearby university. After rounds Sister would, no doubt, allow these would-be medicos to practise their arts on a few willing patients who were by now on the mend and could appreciate the experience as a kind of entertaining therapy.

Somehow the horde walled in Divina Carlyon as she lay propped up in bed, with Sir Vivian and Sister on one side and Doctor Devon with the housemen on the other.

'Well, my dear,' boomed Sir Vivian. 'How vewy nice to see you. Are you comfy? Are they tweating you wight?'

Divina said with a smile, as one old campaigner to another, 'I think everyone has been wonderful, Doctor. I don't know about the rest of the hospital but you can be proud of this ward.'

Magda, behind Sister, and hampered by the trolley, didn't see how, in the time it takes to tell, Sir Vivian's stethoscope had travelled over the patient's thin chest and back.

'Another satisfied customer,' beamed the consultant. 'But you've been vewy naughty, my dear, and neglected yourself. You're too thin and have become anaemic. Now we're going to build you up, give you iron injections and I want you to pwomise you'll eat the high pwotein diet I'm ordewing for you. It may be foul by the time it weaches you, this isn't the Witz, but twy, eh? Twy for me?'

'I'll do anything I'm told,' Divina said obediently.

Sir Vivian bore down next upon Granny Benston, demanding, 'What happened to that stwapping gweat sailor gwandson of yours, then, my dear? Did he knock the Army feller out? Used to box myself,' he told the ward, 'had a gweat time, long weach but no gweat weight; kept 'em all at a distance and bloodied their noses. Made 'em so mad. You're fine, my dear,' after the stethoscope had been busy again, 'clear as a bell. We're going to let you twot along to the toilet for a week, and then we'll think about going home, eh?'

'Another week, Doctor? I feel fine. Don't you need the bed?'

'Not so urgently, my dear. Your legs are going to feel wobbly for a bit and I'd wather they wobbled here than at home, where a young, energetic girl like you might fall and break her hip. You wouldn't like it a bit on Orthopaedic, dear. Tewwible place. Twust my judgement, eh?'

The procession wound on leaving happiness and reassurance in its wake; even the very sick felt better for being visited by Sir Vivian, who rarely mentioned their actual complaint but remembered a husband's name or the size of a family or even an absorbing interest. He gave several patients their discharge while personally appearing to regret their going.

'I shall miss you,' he told Mrs. Thewell, 'but please don't forget my socks. Twelve inch feet. My wife will shwink 'em in no time.'

At twelve-forty, ten minutes' late, Sister Golightly told Magda she could go and to remember to be back promptly at 5. Magda was intending cutting lunch. By the time she had changed and made the journey to Paddington, Stanley's train would be almost due. She groaned as Divina called, 'Oh, Nurse—!' Magda paused politely, perhaps too politely for such a perceptive person as the actress, who said, 'Oh, dear, I'm probably delaying you, or something.'

'I'm meeting a friend off a train just after two,' Magda said with a smile. 'I'll be back at five. But there's just time to tell me how last evening went. Did your daughter come?'

'Oh, yes, and she's so pretty. She wants to go on the stage, would you believe it? Adrian arrived just as she was leaving, I don't think he understands the girl too well. His only concern was appearances. He wants me out of here. He's making inquiries about private Nursing Homes. I don't know what to do about that. I feel I was re-born in this bed and don't really want to leave it. But I mustn't keep you. Eddie's coming tonight. You'll be here by then?'

'Oh, yes. I'm on late duty.' She didn't know how her second meeting with the actress' protégé would go. Personally she would like to berate him for his revealing statements to the Press, but must not make such things her business. In any case she had other things on her mind at present and they were beginning to weigh heavily indeed.

She walked towards the Underground through teeming and uncaring, impersonal Darfield Park. She passed a playground where every breakable thing had been broken. Swings hung by one chain and a roundabout dipped at one side. A couple of big boys, one already showing signs of an incipient moustache, were dicing with death by see-sawing standing up, each trying to bump the other off violently. Probably they were playing truant from the nearby giant comprehensive school and were a part of the problem which must exist in such an area. Maybe their mums were in hospital? Who knew?

On the main road was the cheerfulness of supermarkets and greengrocers' shops with their brightly polished wares. There were crowds of shoppers, too, of all colours and nationalities. Delightful piccaninny children trotted at their mothers' heels in warm, bright English woollies and there were Pakistani women wearing cardigans over their native cotton pyjamas. A pet-shop revealed a doleful puppy sitting shivering in the window with running eyes, obviously sickening for distemper, and, sharing the same straw, a cat with her litter, whom she was suckling while she attempted to make her toilet with great dignity.

Once in the train Magda had her first and only attack of claustrophobia. She wanted the doors to open so she could dash out and run and run for ever. Reason prevailed, however, and she made the one required change and arrived at Paddington in time to decide hunger was causing her to feel weak. She bought and ate a limp, tasteless ham sandwich and drank a cup of grey liquid she didn't recognise as tea. Then she heard the Devon Express announced and stood at the back of the platform, so she could see Stanley before he saw her, ascertain if he looked mad or peevish at having his holiday interrupted like this.

She might have known, though. Stanley could not be read. He stood puffing at his pipe waiting to be claimed by her as though nothing was amiss with his world. He smiled normally as they met but didn't offer to kiss her. She knew he didn't like fusses in public places but a sixth sense told her he wouldn't have kissed her at that moment even had they been in the tunnel of love.

'I'll bet you're wondering why I sent for

you, Stanley?' she ventured.

'Well, you're going to tell me, aren't you, Magda?'

'We can't talk here,' she said.

She ordered a lager and he a pint of bitter. 'I had a second breakfast on the train,' he confided. 'Are you hungry? They do nice pork-pies here.'

'No, thanks. Stanley, I—'

'Yes, my dear?'

'Oh!' the lager slopped as she set it down. 'Why have you always to be so nice? Why can't you say something like "Why have you dragged me here in the middle of my holiday? Why couldn't whatever it is have waited?"'

Stanley mopped up the lager with a tissue; he always seemed equipped to deal with any emergency, producing sticking-plasters, antiseptic pads and styptic pencils at the drop of a hat. His copper-beech coloured hair was plentiful but receding and he made no attempt to hide the shiny bald spot on his head: his moustache was thick and drooped a little like that of a walrus. His light brown eyes looked faintly disturbed by her outburst.

'I can't be what I'm not, Magda,' he now told her. 'I came at your request

107

because I sensed it was a matter of some urgency that could not be discussed over the 'phone. I gather it to be some development regarding our arrangement. Correct me if I'm wrong.'

'Yes, Stanley. I want to break our engagement.'

'I thought you might. I was prepared for that. You've met somebody else?'

'No, I haven't, Stanley. In just over a week? You must think I'm an impulsive fool.'

'Sorry! Then am I to know why?'

'I told you about Jon, didn't I? I mean we were quite frank with each other from the start.'

'True. But you can't exist in the past. First love is notoriously Elysian in character.'

'It just so happens that Jon Devon is the Registrar on my ward. He was as amazed to see me turn up as I was him.'

'I—see,' the two words were long drawn out as Stanley sought to hide behind his pipe which had gone out and took a lot of coaxing back to life. 'So you are continuing where you left off?'

This time he did not attempt to mop

the slopped lager as she put her glass down sharply.

'No, we are not. A lot of water has flowed under many bridges and he has, of course, dallied elsewhere along the way. We have talked, naturally, but nothing else. I only know I can't offer you what I felt for him and it seems mean to give less. I know there is no chance of it but I could love him as intensely again. I had only to be near him for five minutes to realize that. Hearing about his other girl friends has been hell.'

'Does he know about me?'

'Not yet.'

'Then—if it helps—I release you unconditionally. I should hate to stand in the way of true love.'

'Oh, Stanley, you're wonderfully understanding—but I'm not asking you to let me go so I can return to him. His name's linked with one of the hospital sisters who's both pretty and popular. I don't think he regards me as a possibility for the future so much as a casualty in his past. But I was forgetting you within hours of meeting up with him again and that made me feel very bad.'

His hand came over and lay across hers

for an instant. 'That really hurt,' he said, his hazel eyes blinking. 'But thank you for being so honest.'

'I'm sorry, Stanley. I'm too fond of you to want to hurt you ever again.'

'You're not to worry about me. I'll be all right. I'm an old hand at being on my own. Most of the time I like it. I would probably have proved to be irascible as a husband, telling you to leave my socks and shirts alone.'

'You couldn't be irascible if you tried, but thanks for trying to make me feel better.' She groped in her coat pocket. 'I suppose you should have this back'.

The half-loop of diamonds set in platinum slid into his vest pocket among the styptic pencils and plasters. She felt she had no right to warn him not to lose it.

'What will you do?' she asked. 'Go home?'

'No fear. I shall return to Devon and continue my holiday. There's a fast train at four.'

'Oh, good! I'm on duty again at five.'

'I think I'll go for a brisk half hour's walk before all that sitting down again,' he said. 'There's no need for you to come. I'll just say goodbye and good luck.'

She felt his lips brush her forehead like a benediction.

'Do we—keep in touch?' she asked brightly. 'Write and—and so forth?'

'Good lord, no! We wouldn't know what to say. We get on with our separate lives. O.K.?'

She cradled her lager-glass like a chalice as Stanley left her in the pub alone. She deliberately didn't watch him go but she knew the minute he had left. She felt as though she had lost a limb.

★ ★ ★ ★

Jon Devon refused to discharge Divina Carlyon for at least seven days, and when Adrian Byngham had been closeted with the young physician for half an hour he no longer argued. He went back to Brussels and the actress was relieved.

'Some fancy place in Surrey,' she said, 'where I would have a private room and be lonely. I like it here, where I can see everybody and hear all the gossip. But I suppose I'll have to give way to somebody else when I'm well enough to be moved. By the way, what did you think of Eddie?'

Magda privately thought the young man a creep, but answered, 'I can imagine him attracting the opposite sex. Did he explain why he let the gutter press have all that phoney gen about you?'

'But of course. They got it all wrong. Put words into his mouth and then printed what they wanted to.'

Magda forbore to add that they had probably lined the actor's pockets pretty well, too. Divina had resolutely decided against telling her side of the story, and things were quietening down almost to normality on Victoria Ward.

For a day or two Doctor Devon had flitted in and out of the ward, giving his attention to the more seriously-ill patients, usually in the company of Sister, and flitted out again. Nurse Everard, who was like the ward's personal and private newspaper, had it that the male medical ward was keeping him occupied with the rare occurrence of two brothers and one of their sons all very ill with an unidentified virus. Nobody questioned this, but as nobody was dangerously ill on Victoria at that time it could well have been that the registrar was better employed elsewhere.

Magda felt herself to be in a state of

hiatus: she had finished with Stanley and anomalously missed him. She would find herself feeling in her uniform pocket for the ring, and on not finding it sense a quick flutter of panic. She met Doctor Ken Orrey in the canteen one coffee time and found herself agreeing to meet him in the George for a drink that evening. She didn't know what she was letting herself in for but anything was better than being lonely and bored.

It was Saturday and she had been at Darfield Park just a week: It seemed more like a lifetime. Once again she was released for two hours in the afternoon and decided to do domestic chores like washing tights. She had returned to her room regarding the crinkled skin of her hands when a tap came on her door. 'Come in!' she called.

Meg Dixon appeared, rather shyly, and said, 'I saw you come in. Do you think I'll do?'

Magda looked at the exquisite little figure in a close-fitting two-piece turquoise suit with shining dark hair and eyes and asked, 'Do for what?'

'You know I'm going out with Bill Trevelyan this afternoon. I told you.'

'Oh. Then you look fine. Absolutely fine.'

'Fran's not speaking to me. Oh, hell, Warren! What am I going to do?'

'You're either going to have an "affaire" with a married man or get hurt, Meg. You're old enough to know what you're up to.'

'Yes, I suppose I am. Before this I always felt I would be sensible about my love life. Do you believe that? But when it happens sense seems to have no part in it. I sometimes wish my time away in desperation. I wish it was some time next year and something was concluded. Anyway, I mustn't pester you with my problems, though I do regret getting old Fran so worked up. I'm off. I'm committed. Oh, God!'

NINE

Magda paused at times during the evening to wonder if she was really in the saloon-bar of the George public house, or on another planet. She was so out of her element that she felt she had been mad to accept Ken Orrey's invitation. He was obviously the life and soul of the party, surrounded by a group of brash nurses in company with medical students and other young and lively housemen, while she sat alone at a table for two and sipped half a pint of beer. She had travelled with Ken in his old but serviceable M.G. and only in the pub car-park had he given her an idea of what was expected. Before she could open the car door he pounced and they were having a struggle which would have done credit to any wrestling match. As quickly as she fastened buttons he had them undone again, he drowned her protestations with a hungry mouth which caused her almost to suffocate. Having finally got one hand free she slapped him hard and—fortunately where it seemed to hurt.

'Now, listen!' she said grimly. 'I've heard you were a wolf but I would never have believed anybody could be quite so crass. Is a girl supposed to enjoy being assaulted like that? Where did you learn your masculine approach? In a bull ring?'

'Oh, God! One who makes a fuss,' Ken complained, getting out of the car sulkily on his side. 'A kiss me tender, kiss me true, girl. There just isn't the time in a day to make all the right approaches. If it's a drink you want—come on!'

It had been in Magda's mind to walk back there and then, but she realized she had asked for what she had got so far and to try to be adult about it. She nodded to one or two people from the hospital she knew vaguely and then had a half of beer thrust in front of her before Ken became the centre of a livelier throng.

Perhaps he thought he was punishing her by leaving her alone, but she found herself relaxing. Some people like the atmosphere of pubs, but they were alien places to Magda.

'Excuse me,' the young man said for the second time, 'but do you mind if I sit here?'

She gazed up blankly into the homely countenance of the intruder, noting his heightened colour, his glasses and the blinking grey eyes behind them.

'Why?' she asked, indicating that there were other places where he could sit.

'Because I would like to talk to you, if you don't mind. I was there at the bar with Winnie—a friend of yours, I believe,

116

and my ex-fiancée—and she pointed you out to me. Then she said she was going, had had enough of my company and never wanted to see me again, and walked out. I—I don't know how to handle her, and I—I thought you might be able to help.'

'You're George, I take it?' Magda said politely.

'That's right. George Whale.' He held out a hand which Magda clasped briefly.

'How can I help you, George? Surely your business with Winnie can be none of my concern?'

'She did tell you, I suppose, the awful thing I did?'

'About you not turning up on the wedding day? Yes, she did. That was pretty grim if you really loved her.'

'I know. It was panic. Sheer panic. It literally paralysed me. We had made all the arrangements to have a quiet wedding, just her parents and mine, and then it got bigger and bigger until over two hundred were invited, mostly her relatives and family friends. She knows I'm shy and I appealed to her at the last moment to run away with me without telling a soul. I got my asthma, which proved how agitated I was, and when she told me we couldn't change anything at that stage I felt really ill. The chaps in the bank, where I work, wanted to give me a stag night but I just went to my flat, took my effedrine and went to sleep. It was late when I woke and I didn't want to move; I knew something big was supposed to happen but I wasn't up to it. I put my oldest clothes on and went for a walk. That evening I 'phoned Winnie and I told her I wanted her, as much as ever, but not in the big, public way she'd planned. She slammed the 'phone down. I just wanted to die.'

Magda almost reached out and stroked him as he lowered his head, but forbore just in time.

'But you've got together again,' she said encouragingly, 'as tonight proves. I think she's just playing you up a bit, to get her own back, maybe.'

'Do you think so? When I 'phoned her up asking if she'd like to join me for a drink—she only takes a shandy, you know—she said she'd see how she was fixed by this evening. When she arrived I was out of my mind, but she was very cool, almost cold, and seemed to want to talk about the people here she knew, such as which doctor worked where and the wards the nurses were on. "And there's a friend of mine over there," she said, pointing to you. "We started on the same day, though, naturally, I hadn't expected to see the place again." After that she said she was leaving and I was *not* to pester her.'

'Can't you just—forget her?' Magda asked.

George looked at her like a wet spaniel. 'I love her,' he said. 'It didn't happen the way it did because we didn't love each other. It was—oh—other people. So many other people.'

'I can understand how she feels,' Magda said, 'Waiting at the altar, not believing such a thing could happen to her, and then the realization that it had and all these people you speak of looking on. It must have been hell for her. She can't just forgive you, George. You could do it again. You have to win her all over, and don't ask me how to do that because my own affairs aren't exactly in such good order that I can give advice to the love-lorn. I know she defends once in a lifetime love, when we get round to talking of such things, and you come out rather well at times like that. I should play things down a bit, neglect her for a while and then send her roses; remember her birthday—things like that—let time heal.'

'Come on!' came Ken Orrey's voice. 'I'm on call tonight so I must get back. What's this you've picked up, a barnacle?'

George Whale rose and puffed out his chest. He was quite tall and built like a gorilla.

'If you want a broken nose, mate, just say something like that again.'

Magda warmed to George. She determined to do all she could in her power to influence Winnie to give him another chance.

Back at the hospital there was another brief wrestling match as goodnights were said.

'Honestly,' said Doctor Orrey, with the original snow-maiden in his arms, 'I can't say thank you for a lovely evening. What are you frightened of? Did nobody tell you what little boys are made of?'

'Sorry to be a disappointment,' Magda said. 'You can cross me off your list, now, can't you?'

'Just a moment—' an arm came out and grabbed her as she would have turned away— 'are you trying to be funny?'

'You're hurting me,' she told him.

'Oh, really?' a pinch which made her wince.

'Is that you, Nurse Warren?' Jon Devon's voice came clearly. 'I would appreciate a word with you. Goodnight, Doctor.'

'Well?' Magda asked, as they neared the Nurses' Home. 'What is it?'

'Nothing particularly,' her heart sank, 'I just thought you were having a spot of bother. You should be O.K. now, and watch the company you keep.'

She glanced into the sitting-room where nurses were playing chess, knitting, reading, or watching Match of the Day on T.V. Fran saw her and pounced.

'I wonder what she's doing?' she asked worried.

'Who?'

'Meg. Who else?'

'Oh, lord, Fran, I can't worry about anybody else's love affairs tonight. I'd like to go to bed and worry about myself, for a change. Will you excuse me?'

'Sorry I spoke,' Fran shrugged offendedly.

'Honestly,' said Magda in the lift. 'She's probably having the time of her life, so why should we worry?'

Her room was next to Fran's, however, and she heard her pacing about long after the rest of the home was silent. Magda had a day off on the morrow so no need for early rising, but she was concerned to hear Fran leaving her room at well after midnight. When Fran returned, trying to walk silently on big, awkward feet, she found Magda waiting in her dressing-gown.

'What's up? Can't you sleep, either?'

'Not with a pacing tiger next door. Any news?'

'No. She's not back and she's the only one missing. Sister's doing her nut.'

Magda silently thought, 'Oh, no! she's not spending the night with him or anything like that? Aren't men absolute hell!'

It must have been almost two when she finally slept, and it was protestingly that she was aroused by Kitty, the maid, with a cup of tea at a quarter-to-seven.

'Here you are, Staff-nurse. Wet your whistle.'

'Oh, Kitty, I'm off duty.'

'Well, then, you can drink up and have another forty winks, can't you? Want your breakfast in bed? We only do toast and marmalade and coffee, but you're very welcome.'

'Very well, then.'

Having been thoroughly roused up, by having to make such a decision, however, Magda found that further sleep eluded her. She could hear those of her colleagues who were on duty as usual hurtling to and from the bathrooms, calling to each other and bewailing the fact that they would never be ready in time.

There was never enough time for a busy nurse, Magda pondered. From the earliest days of their probation they scuttled about murmuring, 'I'll never get done,' and yet managing to do whatever was required of them by hook or by crook.

When a hush had descended over the place, Magda knew that her colleagues had somehow got themselves ready in time and must by now be in the dining-room.

A tap came on the door and Magda called, 'Come in, Kitty!' but it was Meg Dixon who entered and pulled back the curtains.

'I've told Kitty to bring my breakfast in here, if it's all right,' she said, looking out so that the other could not see her face.

'Of course it is. I—I'm glad you got back all right.'

'I was out 'til half past twelve.' Meg

turned somewhat defiantly to regard her. 'Sister had just gone off duty and the night-porter let me in. He took my name and I'm to see Sister at ten. She'll probably report me to the S.N.O. and I'll be in for a wigging at least.'

'A pity,' was all Magda said.

'A pity,' Meg retorted bitterly. 'I'll say it is! The fact that I'll probably be fined is nothing compared with the fact that my date with Bill was an utter dead loss. I would cry if I had any tears left!'

Magda said, 'Do you want to talk about it? You don't have to, you know. Fran might expect your confidences but I don't.'

'Fran gets emotional too easily, but actually she has nothing to worry about. Bill Trevelyan just doesn't know I exist as a woman.'

There was a pause in the conversation as Kitty came in with a tray containing a large coffee-pot, a mound of toast, a dish of marmalade and the serviceable crockery used for the staff.

'Just coffee for me, please,' requested Meg. 'With a bit of luck I'll develop *anorexia nervosa* and slip away from this cruel world.'

'There's no easy way out of difficult situations for an intelligent person like you,' Magda said, 'and you must have at least one piece of toast. What were you doing out 'til half past midnight?'

'Walking the streets, crying, mostly.'

'Alone?'

'Of course, alone. I'd been to the pictures, previously, again alone, rather than come back here and face Fran's questioning. I met Bill, as arranged, and we drove to his mother's flat in Chelsea to collect his children, two girls of six and four. He had given me no explanation of why the kids were there, or even mentioned his wife. In fact during the drive we had talked shop. Then the kids were all over him, "Daddy"—this—and "Daddy"—that—and it was decided we were going to the Planetarium. I thought it would be great sitting in the dark with him like that, but he managed to put the two kids between him and me, and after twenty minutes I had to take the four-year-old to the toilet, and half an hour later the other one, and so on. In fact the only reason he needed a woman companion at all was to take his children to the lavatory. After that we all had hot-dogs and ices and took the kids back to Chelsea at six-thirty. They began to ask, "Daddy, stay and bath us," but he said he couldn't, with a sort of hungry look at them, as he had to take Nurse, who had been so kind, back to the hospital. I found myself saying nonsense! I was a big girl and could get myself back to the hospital, and he asked "Really?" and I said of course. So the children cheered and Grandma looked pleased and he insisted on taking me to the Underground. On the way he thanked me again for my help, and mentioned how he liked to spend all the time he could with the kids as his wife was likely to be in hospital for at least another year. I found myself asking what was the matter with her and he said she'd got paralytic polio. It hadn't affected her lungs but her legs were very weak. She might graduate to calipers in time but at the moment she was in a wheel-chair. I said how sorry I was; and I got into the train and tried to turn off my feelings about him. But I couldn't. I just wanted to cry for all my hopes which had to be abandoned, because one can't compete with somebody in a wheel-chair and keep one's self-respect, even if the man in the case was willing. So when I got to Darfield Park I went into the Tivoli and just wept, which made me a bit conspicuous because they were showing a broad comedy, and then when I'd made a thorough nuisance of myself I went out and trailed those awful streets, absolutely unaware of the time. You said I was either going to have an *affaire* with a married man or get hurt. Well, I got hurt. In a way I suppose I'm relieved to know where I stand. The uncertainty was killing me and affecting my job. Now, at least there's still the job.'

'Let's hope it all gets better in time,' said Magda.

'You speak as though you know what it's all about, too,' said Meg, with an odd little laugh.

'Whatever makes you think you are unique?' Magda asked with more emotion than she had intended.

★ ★ ★ ★

Tea was served in the sitting room, on Sundays, for those who were off duty. Only on Sundays was there cake and, perhaps, currant loaf, in addition to the staple diet of bread and jam, and so there wasn't the usual exodus to the canteen. Magda

127

was happy to see Meg and Fran enter the room arm in arm. She thought they might want to be alone but Fran sought her out breezily.

'Meg says she told you all about it, Magda.'

'Yes.' Magda glanced at the pretty one who was looking pale but composed.

'We'll help her to get over it, won't we?'

'We'll do our best.'

'Is that a threat or a promise?' Meg asked wryly. 'When one has had an all-absorbing dream for ages how does one get over it, as you put it? I mean—what takes its place?'

'Try knitting,' Magda said, and she was serious. 'If you're doing a complicated pattern you literally can't afford not to concentrate. By the time you've made three Fair-Isle jumpers all may seem very much better.'

Meg laughed oddly, at first, and then with genuine amusement.

'Thanks, Magda. That's what I needed. A bit of commonsense. Hello, Winnie! Take Fran's chair, she has to get back on duty. Are you doing anything this evening, either of you, or would you accompany me to Church?'

'To Church?' Magda and Winnie Twine asked in chorus.

'People do go to Church,' Meg insisted.

'Yes, I'd love to,' Magda said quickly. 'That's a nice idea.'

'Count me in,' said Winnie, just a little virtuously.

'Say one for me,' said Fran as she turned to go. 'I've had a pretty rough day myself, one way and another.'

TEN

Magda was in charge on Monday as Sister took her day off to attend a wedding, and so she was busy, organizing her staff, doing her own peculiar jobs and working in the office. Sister had made a note that Miss Carlyon 'appeared a little depressed,' and so when she had made a round of the patients she visited Divina with time for a chat on her hands.

'O.K. Miss Carlyon?' she asked, automatically raising the woman with one capable arm and plumping up her pillows with the other.

'Oh, Staff-nurse, how nice to see you back! I think I'm O.K. Still very tired.'

'Any visitors yesterday?'

'Yes. I had Debbie and Eddie together. He made her laugh with tales of stage life. In fact they spent more time chatting to each other than to me.'

'Well, we don't want you talking your head off,' Magda said quickly. 'It's rest, rest and more rest for you. I think we'd better have your visitors in one at a time in future.'

Her heart gave its familiar lift as Jon Devon arrived to ascertain that all was well.

'We're coping, sir. Divina's a bit down in the mouth.'

'I'll have a word with her and maybe give her something. How're you fixed for this evening?'

Her colour came and went.

'In what way, sir?'

'When are you free, Staff-nurse, and would you like to go out to supper?'

'Oh, sir! I'd like nothing better. I can't get away before nine, however.'

'I'll pick you up outside your place at ten past on the dot, so I hope you're a quick-change artiste.'

Her day took off on wings after that. An emergency admission was accepted and dealt with and all meals were served and cleared away on time; Divina, who had been given a mild anti-depressant tablet was sitting up and reading a book and Magda felt she loved her ward, her patients, her job. When she sought the reason for this euphoria she had to admit he wasn't far away at this moment, but apparently while there was life there was hope. Crumbs were better than no bread. She had intended going to bed very early to get eight solid hours of sleep, but by the time she handed over the report to the night staff she flew to the Nurses' Home and her room and was changed into a blue angora dress with a light needlecord coat over it in the time it takes to tell. Fortunately her hair was easy to manage. She removed a couple of pins, put a brush through it and it danced on her shoulders. She went down in the lift and opened the swing doors in time to see the yellow Escort drive up. Fran watched her friend get into the passenger seat with open mouth.

'Now what *is* she up to?' she asked the great outdoors. 'One way and another my friends are a real old trial to me.'

Magda, too, was wondering what she was up to as the car stopped not at a restaurant but outside a block of flats. She was still full of inquiry as Jon opened the passenger door for her to get out and then locked the car.

'Now, where?' she asked.

He took her elbow and led the way inside the building.

'Ah, surprise! Lift's working. Up we go.'

On the fourth floor he rang a bell.

'Do come in,' invited Sister Jane Fulham, looking gorgeous in bottle-green velvet with a deep, lace collar. 'I'm so glad you could come.'

Formal introductions were made by Jon and Jane Fulham said, 'Of course I've seen you around, Staff-nurse, but it *is* a very big hospital.'

'Yes, Sister.'

'Now, Jane, what's cooking?' Jon asked jovially, as Magda, in a positive tizzy, hung up her coat and entered a comfortably-furnished sitting-cum-dining room. A table was tastefully laid for three in one corner, so she was at least relieved that Jon had not sprung her presence at the feast without warning the hostess.

'Curry, as you may have guessed,' said Jane Fulham, busy at a rack of side dishes. 'I hope you like curry, Staff-nurse.'

'Love it, Sister,' Magda enthused, glad they were not to be on personal name terms, somehow. In hospital it was always difficult to be too familiar off-duty. If you were Magda and Jane at a party, it was hard to remember that Sister and Staff-nurse must be rigidly enforced on the morrow. 'Is this your home? I didn't know you lived out.'

'Yes, this is my home. I have been thinking of selling the place and moving back into residence, but Jon is persuading me not to.'

'And do me out of my favourite café?' he asked, giving Sister a quick squeeze which perversely hurt Magda's heart. 'Can I help?' he asked.

'Of course you can. The wine. It should be well-chilled by now. Would you mind passing the pea-nuts, Staff-nurse? Thanks. I think we're about ready. I'll put the gas off, now, and we can have our melon in peace.'

Magda tried to enjoy the meal, which was really delicious, still puzzled by her inclusion in the invitation when it was so obvious that her two companions were fond of each other.

'Wouldn't you have preferred to dine tête-à-tête?' was finally torn from her.

'We can do that anytime,' Sister smiled. 'When Jon 'phoned he'd like to bring you along I was delighted. I mean I do know what you once meant to each other. I hope you don't mind, Staff-nurse?'

'No. Not at all.'

'I don't know how you could bear to let him go, he's such a dear.'

'At the time,' said Magda, 'I don't think we parted thinking how dear we were to each other. There were a great many harsh words exchanged.'

'Oh!' said Sister hastily, 'forget those and only remember the good bits.'

Magda met Jon's eye in a moment of stern communication.

I suppose I'm here, Magda pondered, to show that it's off with the old and on with the new. I'm supposed to approve.

'Are you engaged, or anything, Staff-nurse?' asked Sister, as they indulged in a raspberry sorbet.

'I always wonder what that *or anything* means,' smiled Magda. 'I was engaged but

I broke it off last week.'

Jon dropped his spoon.

'Damn it, Jane! Will there be a stain? I'm a clumsy fool and it's so good, too. Why on earth did you do that, Magda?'

'Well, why on earth did you and Angela—I suppose Sister knows about Angela, too?'

'No, I didn't,' said Sister, kindly, 'but I suppose there have been hundreds, he's so attractive.'

'Well, I just wasn't happy about things, and it turned out to be mutual. Stanley thought I was a bit young and stupid.'

'You're young,' said Jon, 'but I would argue the stupid part. Any chance you'll make it up?'

'Not a bit.'

'There'll be others,' said Sister. 'A pretty and attractive girl like you.'

'She's very ambitious professionally, you know,' Jon said as though this explained all. 'Any man is always up against this job of hers.'

'Oh, come, my dear,' said Sister, stroking his head. 'If a nurse could have her head turned by every good-looking man she meets they'd be piling up the dead in the streets.'

'Now don't you start a rights for women movement here! You're as bad as she is. I suppose your husbands will just have to let you work it out of your systems.'

'Of course, Jon. You know I'll carry on whatever happens.'

Magda insisted on helping with the washing up and Jon dried. Sister put her shining Delft away in various cupboards and plumped up the cushions.

Magda put on her coat discreetly while Jon kissed their hostess goodnight.

'Goodnight, Staff-nurse,' Sister said then. 'Do come again.'

In the car Jon said, 'So you're free? Or did you drop him for somebody else?'

'I don't like to think I dropped him. I was very fond of Stanley. I concluded I wasn't in love, and please don't laugh. I know I'm old-fashioned in lots of ways.'

'There's nothing laughable about being in love. It's a damn' good basis for any relationship.'

'Sister Fulham's very nice, isn't she?'

'An absolute peach. Did you enjoy supper?'

'I did indeed. I liked the flat, too. If ever I make Sister I'll consider living out.'

'You're still not thinking you might get married, then?'

'To whom? Excellent prospects don't exactly hang on trees, you know.'

'Oh! I didn't know you were considering marrying an ape. Well, here we are at your front door. See you tomorrow, then.'

'Oh? Where?'

'On the ward, where else?'

'Of course. I'd forgotten for the moment that we work together.'

She didn't know what sort of an evening she'd had when she thought about it. The meal had been good, the company excellent and so careful not to make her feel an intruder, yet there was something decidedly odd in sitting there watching acts of tenderness between two people who should surely have revelled in being alone. Why had Sister Fulham been so anxious to sing Jon's praises to one who had known him so well? Did she want to be sure Jon had no hidden vices another woman might well have mentioned?

Let them go ahead and be happy, she thought as she climbed the stairs, suddenly feeling very tired and weary. Just because you lost out on real happiness, don't begrudge other people the pleasure.

She almost groaned as she saw Fran standing guard.

'Now what's going on, Warren? I saw you with my own two eyes getting into Doctor Devon's car and going off with him. Poodle-faking the other night, too. There are some of us who like right to be right and Sister Fulham is very popular here. We won't have her messed about by anybody.'

'Now look here!' Magda blazed. 'If it's any business of yours I've just had supper at her flat. I like things to be right, too, and having a private detective on my track isn't what I either expect or approve. So shut up and goodnight!'

She ignored the anxious tapping on her door after she had closed and locked it and fell into bed, eventually, wondering what fate had brought her to Darfield Park and a reunion with her past fiancé. What might it have been like, by now, had not Jon Devon bustled on to the ward, all sharp-tongued and officious, on that first day? She would never have considered asking Stanley to release her, in fact the prospect of being his attendant nurse in general practice had definitely attracted her. But life could not be lived by if onlys and just imagines. Life was a day to day business of weaving a pattern as a spider does a web. No one was to say how it would develop or whether the weft or warp would take precedence at any one time. The next morning she started her weaving by apologising to Fran for her tantrum before that young lady could speak. It was better to be friends with one's contemporaries or atmosphere was quickly created. When Meg asked what Sister Fulham's flat was like she knew they had been talking about her.

'Oh, very nice and modern; bright colours, comfy furniture. I believe, for Darfield Park, the view is marvellous, but it was dark, of course, while I was there.'

'I'd like my own flat,' dreamed Meg. 'Fancy being able to get away from all you lot.'

'How does a Sister manage it?' asked Winnie Twine. 'I know they get more than us but not to that extent. George and I were going to buy our own place but it was taking all we'd got, even with the bank behind him.'

'Now how did George get into this conversation?' asked Anne Gideon.

'Come on! Time to slog!' decided Fran.

'I would like to announce that I may have a date on Wednesday with a certain path lab technician. Now if I do I'll need everybody's help on the night. Who can do hair?'

'I'll do your hair,' offered Magda, smilingly. 'I'll make you look so beautiful you'll go off with your lab technician and come back with the Prince of Wales.'

'I should be so lucky,' Fran decided, and they all dispersed their different ways.

ELEVEN

The days passed busily and after Sir Vivian's latest round several faces which had grown familiar, including Granny Benston's, left the ward to be replaced by strangers who were acutely ill and had to be carefully watched.

Nurses were not supposed to have favourites, but everybody loved Granny Benston, for while she was very ill she had always been afraid of being a trouble, and when she had turned the corner she was cheerful and full of a kindly philosophy, encouraging those all around her. Once she was allowed to leave her bed for short intervals, she had tried to help where she could, and had to be physically restrained from joining the domestics in the kitchen, where she insisted she felt more at home.

A great friendship had sprung up between her and the ex-actress, and when Father Christmas, in the shape of Grandpa Benston, had come to collect his wife, his white hair shining like floss and his ruddy countenance all aglow with happiness, she had been sitting by Divina's bed, which was now at the far end of the ward, fully dressed and holding the other's hand.

'This is my Daniel,' she proclaimed proudly. 'Goodness knows how he's managed without me! I'll bet we're in a pickle, and no mistake,' but she smiled fondly as she said it. 'I'm just coming, Daniel. I was saying goodbye to my friend, here. She's leaving, too, tomorrow.'

Magda, who was dealing with a new patient in the next bed, behind drawn curtains, pricked up her ears. She hadn't heard anything definite about Divina since she had been allowed to leave her bed and try out her legs and appeared to be enormously physically improved, as heart

141

cases do behave by going into remission sometimes for years.

Nurse Dewhurst had been sent off duty suffering from a heavy cold.

'I was allride 'til they gave me that anti-flu jab,' she had complained; all staff had the injection in Autumn to counter 'flu epidemics, but a certain number did appear to fall prey to the virus they were trying to overcome. With a nurse short it was hectic even trying to cope. The powers that be to ease the situation, no doubt, had sent two young nurses from the Preliminary Training School to 'help out' but, in spite of their earnestness and willingness, Magda could find them nothing to do which hadn't to be supervised by herself, so that her services to the ward were hampered. They looked so young and made her feel positively archaic. They wore the lavender dresses of P.T.S., which made them look like shy little violets, and caps, at peculiar angles.

'Staff-nurse,' they said, with a kind of reverence, 'what shall we do now? We've finished the drinks and washed up.'

Magda sought to invent a job so that she could get on with her own work without hindrance. Even Sister was on the ward, making beds with Nurse Everard, while Murton was excused for coffee, proving that she had forgotten nothing of the practical side of being a nurse by making the junior work hard and fast to keep up with her.

'Please re-arrange the flowers, Nurses. They look as though they've been thrown into the vases this morning, which they probably have.'

Sister called, 'Staff! Do you think you could find time to chaperon Miss Carlyon taking a bath when you've a moment? She's leaving us tomorrow, as you may have heard, for a private clinic.'

'I'll try to fit it in this afternoon, Sister. I'll get her clean things out, now, and put them on the radiator.'

Divina said, as Magda fished about in her locker, 'Well, hello, stranger!'

'I suppose you think I deserve that, but you must have noticed we *are* rather busy. Anyhow, I'm helping you have your bath this afternoon. See you then.'

Thus it was that Divina brought her story up to date as Magda drew a bath, saw her patient safely into the dettol-fragranced water and then slid into the background, wiping down basins and metal fittings.

'Adrian has laid it all on and insisted it's better for Debbie not to have to come to an area like this, where she could be mugged or raped or—or anything. Adrian is really quite a snob, you know. Anyway, I have to consider Debbie, who is inclined to rebelliousness. She's over eighteen and thinks she knows it all. The publicity I received made her very difficult to handle. She had been carrying a torch for me against her father and grandparents all these years and suddenly I was made to appear no better than a whore, so when she first came here I was something of a freak. However, now she understands that newspapers publish eighty per cent innuendo and only twenty per cent fact, and I've assured her I've done nothing of which she need feel ashamed. It is practically certain that Debbie will live with me at the flat while she studies at the R.A.D.A., which is her ambition. I suppose my experience will come in handy and I can certainly help her prepare for examinations. So something has come out of all that unfortunate business of mine; I have my daughter back again. Eddie has only been in to see me once since he was forbidden to come evenings, but what I once felt for him is quite, quite dead. So I'll be gone tomorrow, Nurse, and I shall miss you.'

'Oh,' Magda was now holding out a warm wrap to receive the bather before making her sit down on a chair nearby, 'you'll soon get used to your new nurses.'

'*You* won't miss me at all, will you?'

'Of course I will,' Magda said promptly. 'I was a new girl, here, and you were my first special patient. I'll miss you, but I won't have the time to dwell on it, if you know what I mean?'

'Of course. I suppose you're not allowed to have truck with ex-patients?'

'We're allowed to have truck with anybody we like. But most ex-patients forget the importance of a hospital ward when they're back in the world again. That's natural.'

'I'll leave you my address and I'd like you to come and see me. You and—maybe—Doctor Devon. I shall never forget either of you. If I was a writer I'd like to dedicate a book about a hospital to you both. You must be shining examples of such a community.'

'Oh! go along with you. We have a job to do. If you catch a chill I won't be doing mine properly, so if you're quite dry put on this warm nightie and dressing-gown immediately. I hear the tea-cups rattling so it looks as though we'll just be in time if we're lucky.'

She did not tell Divina that she would not be on duty on the morrow. It would look a little too pointed and sentimental to mention such a matter.

* * * *

Fran Briscoe popped into Magda's room looking desperate.

'I say, have you a spare pair of tights, old thing? I've just laddered my one and only.'

Magda obliged and continued reading. Fran was back in five minutes, however.

'Do you think you could do my hair again, like on the first time I went out with Derek?'

'Certainly,' Magda obliged, smothering a sigh, 'and may I remind you that you're the one who's having all the fun at the moment?'

'It hasn't quite got to the fun stage, yet, but a girl can keep hoping. Derek's inclined to be a bit serious about his work and takes it with him. On our last date I heard all about how he worked for his City and Guilds finals by keeping his mother, accompanied by eternal nourishment, locked out of his room. Still, he *is* a feller, and I'm learning to be a good listener. Thanks! I suppose I'll do?'

'If you're only listening you'll do fine,' and Magda smiled as the other sped off.

Autumn had slipped into December and the air was suddenly thin with frost and soured by chemicals without a wind to blow their taint away. Patients had come and gone. In only one week there had been four deaths on Victoria Ward.

Having an evening indoors, and wanting to be quiet, meant retiring to one's room. Downstairs the T.V. was roaring away showing an old American detective series and Magda had noticed a couple of coloured nurses using the floor at the back of the lounge for a pattern cutting out session.

She spent a lot of time alone and didn't mind that. She was an avid reader and liked to keep up correspondence between home and friends. Her letters read a little like a diary, a very dull diary: to nurse friends she wrote of her patients and the treatments, how the consultant favoured this drug and the registrar another, and how the most ill patients were always the least complaining and those in under observation a positive nuisance. Her friends wrote back in much the same vein, though they were more forthcoming about the idiosyncrasies of their senior staff. Magda didn't like to say much about Jon Devon, and as some of her friends at Huntingdales might remember him he was always just the registrar. She would hate them to know, who had seen her at nineteen flying to meet him for their evenings off together, when he was coming to the end of his houseman's contract, that they had met up again and spoken casually about subsequent love affairs, and that he was contentedly involved in the present—with somebody else.

This rankled most of all with Magda. Seeing him again had knocked her world into a cocked hat: She had become aware of having lived for three years without total awareness: he had the power to tear veils off things for her, to make every emotion sharp-edged and every patient under his care a very special person. Since the evening they had supped together at

148

Jane Fulham's flat she had found meeting up with him was difficult; she could not feel easy and—not understanding why she did it—she grew prickles like a hedgehog, only they grew inward, too, and hurt. At first he had been almost jovial as though, having taken her into the new world of his intimacy, she could share his happiness. He soon discovered she was defensive in his company, however, and only polite and subservient to a degree which was not quite insolent, and as approachable as an elephant with toothache.

He must have become aware that she was spoiling for a row, or that something was rocking her particular boat, on one day when they stood either side of a bed, behind drawn curtains, where the patient lay supine and moaning.

'Oh, come on, Mrs. Waring,' Magda said in a jolly-hockey-sticks voice, 'all that fuss because Doctor's here? You've been as good as gold all night so don't put on an act now, as though you're dying.'

'Mrs. Waring's head's bad again, Staff-nurse. Isn't that so, dear?'

'Yes—oh, yes, Doctor. I'm in agony.'

'Pshaw!' was the noise which emanated from Magda's lips. *'I've* got a headache, and so has Nurse Murton. We're probably starting 'flu, but we're not tucked up all nice and comfy in bed like you.'

'Staff-nurse,' Jon said hastily, 'would you see me in the office? I want to talk to Mrs. Waring alone.'

'But I'm supposed to escort—'

'I do *not* intend to examine her, so there's no need—' there was such a threat in the tawny eyes that she didn't argue further. On the way to the office she tried to tell herself she hadn't been so very awful. Some patients really did lay it on thick as soon as they saw a white coat.

Jon came into the office, his face livid, making her feel so nervous she wanted to run for it. He came towards her so that she backed and said, 'What have I done? Don't you dare touch me!'

'Only to—' he had seized her shoulder and turned her towards the X-ray viewer in the office. He slipped in a plate, turned on a light and asked her to look. 'The inside of our Mrs. Waring's skull,' he said meaningly. '*I* am not a radiographer, *you* are not a radiographer and I must admit that it meant nothing to me until it was interpreted by an expert. This small U-bend here, shouldn't be there at all. It

150

is caused by a tumour of such malignancy that our Mrs. Waring will not see the week out.' Magda swallowed so hard that it hurt. 'Now she may have been as good as gold last night, and she may be in a state of coma by tonight, but in between times, if she feels pain beyond the realms of the morphine I have just injected, and she groans, you will either offer tenderness and comfort as befits your calling or ask somebody else to do it. The dying are permitted to groan. If you were in P.T.S. I'd make you write that down a thousand times. Is that understood?' She nodded numbly. His voice changed timbre, lost its note of menace. 'Now I'm sorry you and the fair Nurse Murton have headaches. Dear me, I am! And I *do* hope you don't go down with 'flu. Perhaps that is what is making you behave so grotesquely of late. I thought you chose to stay in nursing to excel, but if there's one person worse than a sarcastic teacher it's a sarcastic nurse. You ought to be ashamed of yourself. To sneer at a dying woman and compare your own pathetic vapours with hers—!'

'Don't go on,' Magda begged. 'I'm sorry. I'm miserably sorry. I hate myself. Do you want anything more?'

'No. Unless you can tell me why you're all these things.'

'I don't know. People do have off days. Will Mrs. Waring be staying with us?'

'Why do you ask?'

'I wondered if the neuro-surgeon would want her.'

'Not when there's nothing to be done. It is presumed she'll be well nursed wherever she is.'

'She will.'

'Good.'

'Will that be all, sir?'

'That *will* be all.'

It was just after that he went off on two weeks' holiday, and Mrs. Waring died in Magda's arms on the Thursday evening. Sister Fulham did not accompany Jon. Once or twice Magda saw her looking a bit lost; for a popular person she spent a lot of time on her own. On one occasion Magda fancied she had been weeping, and remembered the time at Ah Fong's when she had appeared to be upset.

'Maybe she can't make up her mind to give up her life as a Sister to be a good and dutiful wife,' Magda pondered on that occasion. 'Jon does seem to pick on dedicated women.'

One evening Magda stepped out of the lift and looked round in surprise. Somebody had changed the green carpet to gold, and there were two half-moon shaped tables with yellow chrysanthemums in pots on them in the corridor. All the paint-work was white and she realized she must have got off on the wrong floor.

'Hello, Staff!' greeted Sister Golightly coming out of the lift. 'Looking for me?'

'No, Sister. I must have been day-dreaming. I'm on the wrong floor, am I not?'

'That's probably wishful-thinking on your part, not day-dreaming. You're look-ing forward to the time when you're promoted and this is your home.'

'Is that it?' Magda smiled. 'Then I'd better come down to earth and get back to the slums. Not that it's so bad up there,' she nodded towards the ceiling.

'No, don't rush off. Come and see how the other half lives now you're here. Have a cup of tea out of real china.'

Magda followed Sister to her 'suite', consisting of an attractive bed-sitting room and toilet facilities and a small kitchenette.

'Not bad, eh?' Sister asked, plugging in the kettle. 'We have to leave the curtains they give us but the bedspread's my own and the pictures and ornaments. In fact I'm collecting so much stuff I must remember I haven't taken root here. Do you take sugar and milk? I don't blame you. Nurses need energy. Have a chocolate digestive.'

'It's quite like a little home of your own,' Magda said, feeling quite enchanted. 'I see you've got a stereo.'

'Yes. But not a T.V. Some of us have portable T.V.'s. but they show such a lot of rubbish and we do have a communal lounge if we're so inclined.'

'Why doesn't everybody live in, then?' Magda asked. 'I would like a shot.'

'Yes, well, there are only so many units. The married Sisters live out, obviously, and some do prefer to pool their resources and share a flat. We're charged rent, you know, and we can hardly entertain our friends. As it is you have to sit on the bed to drink a cup of tea.'

'Sister Fulham has a nice big flat,' Magda ventured.

'Yes, well, she pays a nice, big rent. I've only been there once and she was planning to put it on the market, then. I don't know what's holding her up.'

'Well, I must go,' Magda said. 'Thanks

for the hospitality, Sister, and for showing me your home. It's been a pleasant respite.'

She wondered if that was the next step for her, a suite in the Sisters' wing where either she or her visitor would sit on the bed while they shared a cup of tea. Jon was still away and although he was nothing any longer to her but her mentor, she missed him. Suddenly, the idea of going to see Stanley came to her. But after some reflection she realised she just wanted to find out how he was managing without her.

TWELVE

Nature abhors a vacuum, so it is said. Of the coterie of four friends, dissimilar in character but sharing the same needs, only Fran seemed to have a regular boyfriend at present. The beautiful Meg had taken her disappointment over Doctor Trevelyan harshly; she ricocheted back into the throng of lusty young doctors all eager to entertain her, and allowed them to lavish their pay

155

on her without looking any happier for it. She even went out with Ken Orrey. When Magda saw the two disappearing with a super-charged roar she wondered how much Meg would allow before she said no, or if she would say no at all. Meg was back before midnight looking neither ravished nor interested. She simply looked as though she was walking in her sleep. Winnie Twine was playing her own game as puppet-mistress; being the stronger character in her peculiar partnership with George she tugged the strings which brought him running, and either didn't turn up to keep their dates or left early without explanation. With Magda, who had proved she could not squander her emotions, there was a terrible hiatus in her life, and this was the reason behind her decision to communicate with one who had shewn her affection and done her the honour of asking her to be his wife. She told herself she cared about how Stanley was coping, was interested in finding out in an unselfish way. So she set forth on her next off day by main line train to Bexington, a forty minute journey. Naturally she knew the small town well, from past acquaintance, and took lunch at the Crown, deciding to turn up at Stanley's special Tuesday afternoon surgery for children. Though he liked General Practice he had once been attached to a paediatrician and had a good name for understanding and treating youngsters.

Over her Dover sole and vanilla ice she lost her courage, however, and, deciding to call a spade a spade, told herself she was not here for Stanley's sake, but her own. It had merely been a hysterical gesture on her part and—without more ado—she caught the next train back to Darfield Park.

She was walking up the drive to the hospital when she met Jon Devon coming out.

'Oh, welcome back, Sir!' she greeted. 'Have a good holiday?'

'Fine, thanks. Golf proved to be the correct therapy for my clavicle.'

It felt better with him in the offing and yet she acknowledged that he, too, was only a part of her past. She wondered if he was going to see Jane Fulham.

'Why not?' she shrugged. 'I thought of seeking a harbour today, but he's found one. I don't blame him in the least.'

★ ★ ★ ★

Her ward was growing dear to her. The patients changed but she was now quite fond of Everard and her fund of cockney cheerfulness; in contrast Dewhurst's Yorkshire phlegm was just as funny; she plodded heavy-footedly through the days yet never seemed to fall behind in her work; Murton's glamour didn't hide the fact that she was a serious and dedicated nurse; she was proving something to a family who thought she should by now be content with a butterfly existence and the attentions of young Guards' officers; Nurse Chuong, a Chinese Malayan, was the only member of the staff Magda never felt she knew well. She was inscrutable half the time and it was difficult to believe she was actually working unless one could see her at it. She never stayed late on duty if she could help it, as the others were always doing, but once Dewhurst explained that she lived ten miles out in another suburb and cared for her motherless sister and brother as her father worked as a waiter.

'What absolute rubbish!' Sister said on one occasion when Magda made some excuse for the Chinese scuttling off duty.

'She came here from Malaya for training and her father is a doctor and has a private clinic back home. The young madam is just money in the family concern. We had her sister, until she became a senior and was given a ward, and then she said she had to go home as there was sickness in the family. I'll say there is! As a British-trained hospital Sister she's making her fortune back there!'

'Ah! So I'll see that Heavenly Light doesn't put on our accommodating Dewhurst in future.'

'Heavenly Light?'

'That's what her name means.'

'A good thing I found that out before the staff change-over.'

On January first the staff still in training changed wards. Sister and the Staff-nurse were fixtures, for at least a year, and Magda was already regretting losing her flock in anticipation. Still, there was the Founders' Day Dance and Christmas yet to look forward to. It was a frosty December and the wallflowers planted out bordering the walks were shrivelled grey by the cold. Gardeners made bonfires which created leaf-smells, much preferable to the normal stink in the still air.

'You go to coffee, Staff,' Sister ordered. They had just laid a patient out and the trolley had gone off to the mortuary without most of the patients knowing. 'There's no hurry. Don't rush back.'

Magda sought a table at the back of the canteen and queued for her coffee and biscuits, then sat down with the nurse's usual gasp of pleasure at taking her weight off her feet. She wriggled her toes in her flat-heeled sensible ward shoes.

'Excuse me, Staff-nurse—?'

Magda looked up to behold Jane Fulham holding a small tray containing coffee and a piece of pie— 'may I join you?'

The table was for two.

'Please do,' Magda said promptly, moving a newspaper and her purse out of the way.

'I had no breakfast,' Sister said, indicating the pie. 'When one has one's own housework to do meals are inclined to go by the board.'

'That's naughty,' Magda said.

'I'm glad we've met up again,' Jane Fulham said. 'The hospital's so vast you don't meet some people for years. I rather hoped Jon would bring you round to the flat again.'

Magda considered this. 'Perhaps he thinks that three's a crowd,' she decided.

Jane Fulham flushed. 'Yes, of course. I'm sorry. That was clumsy of me. Have you seen him lately?'

'We've just lost a patient. I believe he was on the ward most of the night and certainly until half an hour ago.'

'One has to realize with Jon that his work is of primary importance to him.'

'I've always known that.'

'It's not a bad thing though, is it? If you're sick and you know your doctor will come through hell or high water if you're taken worse—?'

'Jon is certainly rather special like that.'

'And speaking of the devil—?' Jane was now laughing and a shadow loomed over the table. Jon dragged up an empty chair and a waitress brought him a cup of tea and a bun. He was a favourite with most of the staff.

'I've just about finished,' said Magda tactfully.

'Oh, no you haven't,' Jon denied. 'Sister told me she'd given you permission to take a break. Unless I'm interrupting a woman-to-woman chat?'

'No, don't be silly,' said Jane Fulham.

'Then why were you talking about me?'

'Only about your dedication. You don't do enough playing.'

'Darfield Park is rather short of night clubs.'

Jane said, rather nervously, 'Would you two be free together next Saturday evening?'

'Well—' John glanced at Magda who looked quickly away, not knowing what to say. 'I'm free, but why ask? Do you want to play cook, again, and make sure you've got a hungry and appreciative audience?'

'I'm free,' Magda said quickly, thinking she had offended Sister previously by saying three was a crowd.

'Well, then, I'm stuck with two tickets for a concert at the Albert Hall. I bought them from Sister Harker who's a music enthusiast but I now have other plans. I hate to be ten quid out of pocket.'

'How about it, Magda?' Jon asked directly. 'I've only listened to such things on radio, but everybody does seem to be having a very good time.'

'I'd like it, but—' Magda sought for alternatives desperately. 'I could probably get one of the other nurses to go with me if you'd rather do something else, Jon.'

'No. I have nothing else planned and we'll give Jane her ten quid back.'

'No, please,' said Sister, covering Jon's hand with her own. 'It was the waste I minded. I shall be so happy just to have you use the tickets. There they are. They're supposed to be quite good seats.'

'Oh.' Jon smiled faintly. 'I had visions of standing up, throwing balloons and wearing my college scarf.'

'You're too old for that sort of thing and it's not the last night of the Proms but a serious concert,' Jane said rather sharply.

It was Magda and Jon who exchanged glances, sharing the joke.

'Now I have to get back,' said Magda, firmly. 'Thanks for everything. I never expected the bonus of a concert with my coffee.'

THIRTEEN

In what had been Divina Carlyon's bed was a plump woman suffering from pleurisy. She was obviously ill, and in pain, but she was also a moaner. Long after she had been

163

given injections and tablets she was crying out for a higher agency to help her.

'Oh, God! Oh, God! I can't stand this! Why me? What have *I* done? Oh, God!'

Magda approached the patient and asked her, quietly, not to make so much noise.

'It's not you that's suffering, is it?' the other demanded. 'I've been like this for a week, now.'

'Some people suffer for months,' Magda said a little more sharply. 'Now I do know you're having some discomfort, Mrs. Wuff, but shouting is only irritating your lungs. Give the tablets a chance by trying to rest and relax. You're in good hands, now.'

'I don't know about that. I hate hospitals. I have a daughter and you'd think she could look after her own mother. But no. "You're going into hospital, Mum," she says, and here I am. I'll die, I know I will. You bring them up and then they don't want you. Oh, God!'

'Now, Mrs. Wuff, you *must* be quiet. We have patients who are trying to sleep. You're much better off in hospital than with your daughter.'

'Now don't you tell me what's best for me, my girl!' the woman became shrill. 'Everybody knows the reputation of this place, a common, low-down— Oh! the pain!'

Jonathan Devon appeared and drew the curtains round the bed almost sharply.

'Now what's up?' he demanded. 'What's all this row about?'

'I asked Mrs. Wuff to be quiet and—and she won't, sir.' Magda's heart had taken a dip. She seemed to have played an identical scene once before.

'She's bullying me,' moaned the woman, 'saying how lucky I am to be in hospital and me in such pain.'

'Yes, I know it's not very nice to be in pain,' said Doctor Devon, studying the woman's chart. 'Staff-nurse, one tablet Valium, five mgs. every four hours.' He was scribbling busily on the chart as he spoke. He glanced up. 'Start now, stat,' he said, 'then I'd like a word with you in the office.'

So it *is* to be another wigging, she thought, as she tapped on the office door and said 'Yes, sir?' It was Sister's afternoon off. 'I'm sorry if I upset the patient. Her moaning and groaning was disturbing the others and she'd had everything I dare give her. She'd had antibiotics and pain-killers and just kept on and on.'

'Yes, we do get them in all varieties, is that it?' asked Doctor Devon. 'Those with low and those with high pain thresholds. Ours not to reason why. We mustn't make the mistake of thinking some are necessarily braver than others. They just feel less acutely.'

'I'll attend a lecture on the subject when I get the time,' Magda said bleakly.

'Good! I think you'll find that sedating our noisy customer will enable the pain-killers to work and that we'll all get more peace in consequence. I'll pick you up at seven on Saturday. O.K.?'

'Pick me up?' she had to collect her thoughts. 'Oh, yes. But I'll come to the car-park if you like. Is that what you wanted to see me about?'

'Of course. What else?'

'I'll get back to the ward, then.'

She smiled and he remembered her dimples. Soft, bright hair gleaming under a neat cap, grey eyes which reminded him of country rain-pools and a generous, soft-lipped mouth he had often kissed.

'Very well, Staff-nurse,' he said hastily.

166

'Let me know if you have any more trouble.'

Sister almost bumped into her in the doorway.

'Go to tea, now, Staff. You know, Doctor, we've got a good girl there. She's a hard worker and very responsible. Do you agree?'

'A very nice girl, Sister, and, as you say, a good worker.'

'She'll make a good Sister one day. That's if she's sensible and doesn't rush off to get married.'

'Spoken like a true Women's Libber,' Jon teased.

'Oh, I'm not for Women's Lib, Doctor. Women are women and men are men. But I do mind when a good nurse wastes herself, and her training, chained to some kitchen sink.'

Magda knocked, she was carrying a tray. 'I was passing the kitchen and I knew you could both do with a cuppa,' she said, 'just in case Doctor has time to spare.'

'Chained to which kitchen sink, Sister,' Jon Devon asked when she had gone. 'Her own or the Ward's?'

'Oh, go along with you! You know what I mean.'

167

★ ★ ★ ★

Magda found her room had become a kind of rendezvous. For one thing it was in the middle of a corridor equidistant between Fran at one end and Meg at the other; Winnie Twine was just opposite. On Saturday evening they turned up one at a time; Fran, first, who was starting on a spell of relief night-duty, was in uniform and still yawning from the half-sleep of the day before the changeover.

'My! You look glam!' she decided, waking up to regard the other as she sat at the dressing-table wearing a dark brown velvet dress with a cream lace collar. 'Just like Marie-Antoinette before they chopped her head off.'

'Thanks! I'll insist on taking that as a compliment.'

'Oh, it's meant to be. Someone special?'

'Pardon?' Magda was squinting as she put grey eye-shadow on.

'Your date. I presume you're not all dressed up like a dog's dinner for a member of your own sex?'

'Now you're becoming less complimentary and increasingly nosey. I'm going out

168

with an old friend if you must know. A very old friend.'

'Like aged ninety-two?'

Meg entered. She was in a new grey suit and wore her hair up. She looked delicious.

'You, too,' Fran groaned good-naturedly. 'I must have the best looking friends in the hospital.'

Magda glanced in the mirror and smiled at Meg. Fran could not contain herself. 'Who's the lucky man?' she asked at length.

'Your Derek, if you must insist. I'll let you know what I think of him when we get back.'

'But Derek's working. He told me so. He's coming to the ward for cakes and coffee about eleven. You're kidding!' she accused finally.

Meg said, 'Well, you *are* looking nice, Magda. Have a good time. I suppose I should be off, but no harm in keeping them waiting a bit, is there?'

Winnie Twine entered just as Magda had patted her lips dry. She almost groaned.

'Sorry, ladies, but I'm off to a concert and I don't want to miss the overture.'

'I'm having supper with George,' Winnie

announced. 'At least I'll have the main course, I'm hungry, but then I thought I'd make an excuse to go to the ladies' and leave.'

Magda rose and donned her warm camel-hair coat.

'Now don't you think this nonsense has gone on long enough?' she asked. 'George has sinned and he's sorry. He's certainly paid for it. Why can't you enjoy a nice supper right through to the end, talk, make-up and forgive and forget?'

'Hear! Hear!' yawned Fran.

'*You've* never been left in the lurch, have you? Any of you? You don't know what it's like.'

'Not for the lack of telling,' contributed Meg.

'All right. I can see when I'm not wanted. I always thought I could confide in you, Warren. At one time you seemed the sympathetic sort.'

'Well so you can, and so I am. But George confided in me, too, and if I'm sympathetic by nature I couldn't shut him out, now could I? He wanted my advice on how to win you back. If you don't want to be won, Winnie, I really think you should tell him and let him go. He'll recover, finally, and find somebody else. But just to have him tag along to torture doesn't seem right.'

'I'll wait until after the Founder's Day dance. I've asked him to that. One way or another I'll give him my answer then.'

With relief Magda shepherded them all from her room and closed and locked her door. In the car-park Jon was growing impatient.

'I thought you'd forgotten,' he said.

'No. I was giving advice to the love-lorn. Does that make you laugh?'

'Not at all.' He found gear, reversed, and they were away. 'I would simply say physician heal thyself, first.'

'Am I supposed to be love-lorn, then?'

'Perhaps not. You end affairs, don't you? One should feel sorry for the fellows in your life.'

'Oh, they seem to be getting along fine without me. One should never over-estimate one's importance in things.'

'Why did you give up your—Ernest, was it?'

'No. His name was Stanley. I wasn't right for him. He was too nice to be used as a convenience by me. I wasn't in love with him.'

'Eighty per cent of people marry who are not in love in the accepted sense, and sixty per cent are very happy.'

'I do find statistics stimulating, but I can only reply that such a marriage would not be right for me.'

'Or me. It's the devil, isn't it?'

'What is?'

'Waiting for that spark to ignite a relationship.'

'But I thought you—had hopes in that direction?'

'So I do. But the object of my affections remains aloof. Kind, but—aloof.'

'And if she turns you down?'

'We haven't got anywhere near that stage, yet. I'm not sure I stand a chance with her. But if ever we do, and she spurns me, I shan't shoot myself. I have my work.'

Magda's heart was performing strangely in her chest. So it wasn't really on between him and Sister Fulham, then? Well, why not give her a little competition and make her fight for him? Jon should not have to beg any woman for her favours, and *she* should know that if anybody did.

The Rossini overture set the pace of the concert. It was to be jolly and rousing all the way through. The only sad note was introduced by an Italian Tenor who sang of his 'pearly Adriatic and long lost Maria', so that Magda piped a tear.

'I can't stand tenors,' she explained as she borrowed Jon's handkerchief. 'I mean I love them so much it hurts.' The tenor's encore was "Funiculi–Funicula" and even she couldn't weep at that, but clapped and stamped as the audience was invited to do. At the intermission they went to the bar and queued for drinks.

'We'll miss the bassoon solo,' Jon said, as at last they were served and could hear the orchestra tuning up.

'So long as we don't miss the "Pearl Fisher" duet,' Magda said, and clinked her glass against Jon's with a laugh. 'Remember we always said "Prosit" and you told me eyes always had to meet as it was said?'

'Prosit', said Jon, and grey eyes looked into the dark sand of his with a dubious smile. 'We did a lot of daft things,' he remembered, 'but they fitted us at the time. I don't think I've "prosited" anybody else since.'

'Aha!' she said. 'So I'm unique in

something!' She felt she had him just a little intrigued and asked, 'Shall we creep back, now?'

'If you're ready.'

The large, burly man in the second back row was having difficulty breathing. He was obviously a bucolic type but his colour was now that of putty. Jon remembered him in the bar, ordering whiskies, being pressed by his wife to hurry up.

'Do be quiet, James,' she now complained. 'They're all looking at you.'

'Sorry, m'dear. I seem to have this congestion and my arm's heavy. I—'

'You wouldn't have congestion if you didn't swill your drink down so. Now do let people enjoy the music.'

Magda wondered why they were pausing listening to a domestic quarrel. She understood better as Jon leaned sideways and caught the man in his arms as he fell forward, breathing stertorously.

'Come on, Mags! I need help. Let's get him to the back of the hall.'

A couple of men had stood, sensing an emergency, and were helping carry the stricken man out of the auditorium.

'What's the matter?' shrilled the woman

who had lately been railing. 'He only had a couple of whiskies. He's not drunk, is he?'

'Not drunk,' Magda said, and could not resist adding, 'please don't make such a noise. Let the others enjoy the music. Your husband's ill. I'm not a doctor but I have seen a coronary thrombosis before. He needs quiet and care and my friend *is* a doctor, so he'll get both. Please try to help and don't panic.'

'James, with a heart attack? He's never ailed a thing in all his life.'

'That's often the case. Now I'd better help because I'm a nurse. Will you be all right?'

In answer the woman opened her mouth and shrieked.

Jon said, 'For God's sake shut her up,' and rammed two tablets into Magda's hand. With difficulty, as they congregated in the manager's office, she persuaded the woman to take the sedative and then leaned over the man on the floor and mopped the icy sweat from his brow.

'Am I going to die?' he asked.

'No. Of course not. Doctor's getting an ambulance and you'll be right as rain in no time.'

'How will—Kath get home?'

'After we've seen you safe into bed we'll take her. Don't worry about a thing.'

'Right. I won't.'

By the time the ambulance arrived the stranger had died in Magda's arms. Not all the mouth to mouth resuscitation would bring him back to life again. To a blur of figures in white with oxygen apparatus she heard the lovely requiem of the duet from the "Pearl Fishers" in the background and felt she would always remember it so. It had started out such a jolly evening. Why had the nature of their job to make it end on such a grim note?

'Come on!' it was long after midnight and Kath had been seen home, her doctor and the Vicar called and they were driving back to Darfield Park. 'You've met death in many guises in your time.'

'I know. I think a good cry sometimes makes you feel better. He was such a nice man. I'm sorry I'm being so wet.'

'That's O.K.' He reached out a hand and stroked her cheek. 'Have you shut up, now? I can't present you to Home-Sister in tears.'

'Yes. I'm O.K.'

They had 'phoned Home-Sister to

explain the position and why they would be late. Magda was admitted, questioned and asked if Doctor had gone to bed. Of course Sister knew she had been out with Doctor Devon. She hoped she hadn't gossiped to the other nurses.

★ ★ ★ ★

At the breakfast table Anne Gideon said, 'We heard you were held up doing your duty. Is there a doctor in the house and all that'.

'Yes. That's true. It was a coronary and he died within minutes. The patient, that is.'

'Hard cheese,' said Carrie Dale. 'Were you out with Doctor Harvey? He's our cardiac specialist.'

'No, she wasn't,' Meg said quickly. 'Would somebody pass the marmalade down this end, please? Who's seen *Jesus Christ Superstar?* It's marvellous. I don't know what there is about it but it makes you actually feel religious. I wonder if it lasts?'

Magda glanced at Meg who winked. 'Don't tell them anything,' she seemed to say. 'Let them guess.'

FOURTEEN

The Founders' Day Dance was a historical occasion at Darfield Park Hospital, and Magda couldn't quite understand its present-day significance. Apparently it had once been a time when the medical staff honoured the Sisters and senior staff, but a Town Hall function, on almost similar lines, apart from the fact that there was more eating and drinking and less—if any—dancing, had superseded the original which was now given over to the State-Registered Nurses of Staff status.

'It's fun,' Fran Briscoe summed it up. 'The doctors let their hair down without the S.N.Os. or Sisters, there. You wouldn't recognise some of them. But next day they're back to normal, and don't let anybody forget it.'

Magda still had her doubts. Obviously there were going to be a great many more women than men, and those girls fortunate enough to have boy-friends or fiancés outside the hospital were asked to invite them along. There was a buffet, so it was said, which was paid for by the medical staff and no expense was spared to titillate young appetites. There was also a short cabaret, the turns being also provided by the medical staff from among their own numbers.

Magda still felt dubious, like a child being taken to a circus against her will by rich uncles. She said as much to Meg who agreed she had once felt the same way, but it was really the doctors' way of saying thank you and there were really some very nice doctors in the hospital.

'You should see Sir Vivian doing the jive,' she smiled. 'Actually he doesn't realize that went out years ago, but at least he tries.'

So, as usual, on the big night, Magda's room became the rendezvous.

Fran came in wearing a new green-brocade dress and with curlers in her hair.

'That's really smart,' Magda decided. 'I hope that red frock you favoured went for dusters. I like your hair.'

'Now none of your cheek, Warren! That's your job. Where's your frock?'

'It's here on the bed. Just a little cocktail

number. I didn't expect I would be asked to a ball when I did my packing.'

'You'll look smashing,' Fran decided generously. 'You're like Meg. You're built so that you'd look good in a sack. Ready to do me, now?'

Meg came in wearing cherry velvet. She was holding her brow and saying, 'My God! but I've got one hell of a headache. I never felt less like dancing.'

'You're always having headaches, now,' Fran accused. 'How come?'

'I don't know. I probably need glasses, or something. However, I've taken a couple of distalgesics so don't let's despair. Winnie! Hello!'

Winnie Twine was wearing a dress of blue taffeta which looked as though it had been made for her mother. Her straight black hair was unadorned and her spectacles were pale-rimmed, the lenses quite thick.

Thinking of something nice to say, Magda ventured, 'That colour's lovely Winnie. Really lovely.'

'Hm! Actually I have a lovelier dress but I'm not making any effort for George; I invited him and he can take me as I am, or not.'

180

'You could have waved your hair,' Fran said frankly.

'Nature did not endow me with wavy hair, so why should I?'

'Nor did Nature endow you with red lips, but I see you're wearing lipstick.'

'We're not entering for the Miss World Contest,' Meg said pacifically, 'so I suggest we go and make our entrance.'

The Nurses' dining-room had been cleared for the occasion, and as it stood some distance from the wards it was hoped the noise would not disturb the patients. A dais had been erected at one end and there was a great mass of chrysanthemums banked round it. A trio of musicians were trying out their instruments and at the opposite end of the room was a really fantastic buffet serviced by professional waiters.

'Our dining-room maids wouldn't know what to do with real food,' Fran said cynically. 'I suppose it's too early to grab a plate of that smoked salmon?'

'Just a bit,' Magda laughed.

'Come on! We're supposed to say hello to Doctor Griffith, the most senior of our consultants. He prides himself on never forgetting anybody's name. I've been

Nurse Ha-hum for as long as I can remember. Where's Meg gone?'

'Into a corner to let her distalgestic work, no doubt.'

There were, as Magda had foreseen, a great many girls, and all of them prettily dressed and coiffured, apart from Winnie Twine, and the doctors were, to a man, in dinner suits and looked most unfamiliar. A few other young men were present looking, for the most part, out of place.

'You have met, of course?'

'Yes. Hello George!'

'Hello er—Magda. I hope we may have a dance later on. Winnie told me to ask you.'

Winnie tried not to look virtuous as Magda smothered a smile.

'I should be delighted, George. Thanks a lot.'

Magda drifted away to find the room was now crowded. Meg was being chatted up in her corner by the blond doctor from gynae—Hackett, she thought was his name. She seemed to lose interest in their conversation as Bill Trevelyan drifted by. In spite of Meg's recent hedonistic pursuits, was her heart really in this man's hand still?

Magda felt relieved that she had not made the mistake of over-dressing for the occasion, as some of the girls had. The elegant black cocktail-dress she wore was by no means new, but it was one of her favourites. It was mid-calf length, and was slashed to the waist on each side by a silver *lamé* pleat. With it went a short silver bolero, which could easily be discarded if she was asked to dance.

'Well, of course I'm sure of one dance,' she told herself as she walked round, more an interested spectator than a participant at this stage, 'if only with George.'

The orchestra suddenly struck up a waltz and the girls tried not to look too hopefully around them. The paunchy Doctor Griffith sailed manfully on to the chalked floor with the tall Anne Gideon, obviously succumbing to this most important of the 'dwarves' manning the hospital. Magda felt a tap on her shoulder.

'Excuse me,' a fair-haired, serious-looking young man was regarding her. 'I don't think we've met. I'm on the surgical side, my name's Gregory. May I have the pleasure?'

Doctor Gregory was a good dancer and Magda began to enjoy herself. Many of the girls were dancing together and she saw Fran looking deeply into her Derek's eyes while trying not to fall over his feet. Meg passed in the unlikely arms of Sir Vivian Rydale.

'Thank you,' as the waltz finally ended. 'Can I get you a drink?' asked Nat Gregory.

'A soft one, please. Then you really must circulate. What I mean is—' she laughed lightly— 'there are so many of us and so few of you.'

He handed her a glass of grapefruit and said, 'You really are very understanding. Perhaps we can meet again, sometime?'

'Perhaps.' She let this go. She didn't want further complications in her life at present.

The drink lasted her throughout a slow foxtrot and then Meg joined her looking flushed.

'That's the first time I've danced with Sir Vivian and I hope it's the last. He really can't dance for toffee.'

'How's the head?' asked Magda.

'A bit better but my eyes feel funny. I really must apply for a test. Apart from that I'm having quite a good time. I'm beginning to realize that you have to take what's offered in this life, like squeezing all the juice from the orange in your hand and not crying for the pineapple in the window.'

'So long as nobody else gets hurt,' Magda said quietly, thinking of Bill Trevelyan's wife and her unenviable situation.

'You think Lady Rydale might have minded her husband asking me to dance?' Meg asked teasingly.

'No. I didn't mean him.'

'I know whom you meant and it's all over. That's why I can enjoy myself suddenly. I have no ties or fetters and—thank God! no regrets. I suddenly seem to have discovered in myself a capacity for having fun. That may all be changed when I'm wearing glasses.'

'You'll make glasses look good,' Magda said encouragingly, 'and it may not be your eyes at all.'

'Darling?' she heard above them. Ken Orrey was holding out both arms for Meg who rose, was received into a masculine embrace and swept into the throng.

'Darling?' came another voice, on a more quizzical note, and Magda looked up into Jon's face, whose arms were also reaching. He had shaved off his beard and looked as young and handsome as she had ever remembered him. 'Isn't my technique right, or something?' he asked challengingly.

Magda remembered about the orange in one's hand and stood up, slipping out of her bolero.

'Nothing wrong at all,' she said, and slid into his arms. She had been there before, and the magic for her was as of old. Once or twice, during the foxtrot, he held her away to look at her and always she was smiling. She hadn't remembered his tallness, how when they danced she was pressed against his chest, smelling the after-shave, carbolic, man-fragrance of him.

The dance came to an end after being encored and she was unaccountably sorry. After this she would feel herself to be alone in the crowd, no matter who asked her to dance.

'I don't want to be greedy,' he told her, 'but may we have supper together? In about half an hour I'm going to be starving and shall claim you.'

She squeezed the orange a little harder and said, 'I'll be waiting.'

In the meanwhile George claimed his dance while Winnie stood by, beaming.

'She's led me to hope I'm forgiven,' he said, apologising for stepping on her toe. 'She won't name a date but says she'll think about it.'

'That's something, George.'

'But I do find her hard to understand. She seems brittle at times. I wish to God I hadn't got weak knees at the psychological moment. I've told her I'll marry her in a cathedral, if she wants, in front of thousands.'

'I wouldn't push your luck. Just be natural. The brittleness is a shell she's grown. I think only tenderness and understanding will get through to her. But all the best, anyway.'

'Thanks.'

She was glad to find Jon Devon waiting for her promptly as arranged.

'The cabaret's rotten,' he confided, leading her to a small table at the back of the room, 'so if you can't see, you're not missing anything. Now I'll go and get some food. Will you leave it to me?'

'Absolutely. I'm ravenous, anyway.'

There was a rush, now, on the buffet, but eventually Jon reappeared with two plates piled with food, forks in his pocket and Doctor Gregory following behind with a bottle and two wine glasses.

'Will that be all, sir?'

'Yes, thanks, Nat. If you don't pass your exams you can always become a waiter.'

Magda squeezed the metaphorical orange in her hand and made no excuses for enjoying herself. She was here being attended by a very charming and good looking man whose hesitant fiancée was helping to run the hospital at this moment. She wasn't going to look a gift-horse such as this in the mouth a moment longer.

'This is good,' she said, raising her glass to complement the mouthful of smoked salmon she was enjoying. 'Thank you, Jon. Thank you, very much.'

★ ★ ★ ★

Somehow, in the midst of all the pandemonium of the occasion, Jon and Magda just talked. The wine had loosened her tongue and she found herself recalling past events they had shared together, and he, others. The cabaret went on in the background of their conversation, being hysterically received for the most part, but still the two kept themselves apart and in perfect amity.

When the dancing started again she felt suddenly guilty.

'Oh, Jon! I'm keeping you all to myself. You must circulate.'

'Rubbish!' he said promptly, and looked with some disapproval round the room. 'All these candidates for lung cancer should know better and are poisoning the atmosphere. How about a breath of fresh air?'

She agreed and he helped her to find her coat and slip into it. The courtyard outside the dining-room was deserted and the night was cold, turning frosty with the pale eyes of far-away stars winking. The lights of the hospital were now muted except for windows where members of the night-staff were writing up their reports or making their refreshing 'cuppas'. The Accident Wing and Casualty were in full blaze, however.

'Jane's doing a stint on geriatrics,' said Jon, taking Magda's arm companionably in his own. 'Quite a few sisters volunteered to take over for the night.'

They had turned into what passed for a 'garden' at Darfield Park, a few stunted laurel bushes and wallflower plants with their green spikes turned to grey, as though they cringed from the frost.

'Is it too cold to sit?' Jon asked, as they reached a bench.

'Not for a little while,' she answered, and laughed as they huddled together, still arm in arm. 'I suppose we're mad to come out in the cold like this. My knees are knocking.'

'My knees are knocking, too,' he said, and his voice was unsteady, 'and I'm not at all cold. All that remembering we did inside reminded me of other things. Oh, Magda!' He bent and kissed her with a kind of ferocity born of hunger. He reached and she didn't question the demand of his arms, the sudden electrification of a hand touching her throat and the lips exploring hers sending needles of awareness which started somewhere down in her toes and roared through her being until she lost her identity and became just half of something seeking its entirety and almost finding it. She could hear his heart pounding and in his strength her own weakness was a sudden and delicious affliction. She could only bear it by clinging and to cling meant the madness went on, and on.

'Oh, my darling!' Jon crooned. 'It would take such a little encouragement for it all to be just the same again.' He sought her lips again and then the idyll ended as a light flashed on.

'So there you are!' Fran's voice snapped. 'Put the torch out, Ikey-Mo, I think we've seen enough. Sorry to interrupt your capers, Warren, but somebody saw you leave the hall and I thought you just might be interested to hear that Meg's had some sort of attack. She's being examined by Sir Vivian, now. But do carry on, please. I'm sorry we disturbed you. Come on, Ikey!'

Male nurse Finglestein shuffled uncomfortably.

'What does she mean, Meg's had an attack?' Magda asked him, staying him with her arm on his.

'A sort of faint, but she had violent head pains first.'

'I think I'll go and take a look at Nurse Dixon,' Jon said, not referring to the past scene or appearing the least put out. 'Obviously Staff-nurse Briscoe is upset and we must put her mind at rest.'

'Well!' Fran growled as he went on his way, 'I never expected to see you necking with him.'

'And we didn't expect people to come looking for us with torches,' Magda flashed. 'I'm sorry about Meg, but how would you like it if your friends went looking for you and Derek with a torch?'

'My conscience would be quite clear,' said Fran in a thin, high voice, 'because he's my friend. I'm not stealing from anybody.'

'And I am?' Magda asked sharply. 'How do you know that Sister Fulham has any claim on him? That she isn't shilly-shallying and not making up her mind? Good lord! Either she wants him or she doesn't,' and she marched away towards the Nurses' Home in high dudgeon.

Next morning the news was that Meg was in sickbay, quite comfortable but due to be subjected to several tests. At breakfast Magda pointedly avoided Fran and the rest of the crowd and was joined by Winnie Twine, concerned only with her own affairs as usual.

'I thought George was rather sweet last night,' she decided, 'and I practically told him we'd go ahead, again, maybe marrying at Easter. But I've hardly slept all night for wondering if I'm doing the right thing.'

Magda was in a mood to speak her

mind. 'I think you are,' she said. 'You won't do any better, so stop kidding yourself.'

'Oh, I'm sorry. Am I boring you?'

'Yes.'

Winnie went offendedly away. In her place came Elsie Lyons, staff-nurse from Minor Theatres. 'Look here, Warren, I heard about last night.'

Magda's eyes grew hard as pebbles. 'How interesting for you!' she observed.

'Yes, and I'd like to tell you that some of us won't stand idly by and nurture the other woman in our midst. Sister Fulham is too soft and gentle to fight for her rights, but we're quite prepared to do it for her. I know there's an engagement in the offing. She showed me the ring and said it would be quite official when they have a party on Christmas Eve, and that's next week. So you keep out of his way except for when you have to see him on the ward, do you hear? Just so you don't forget we're serious we're sending you to Coventry for a week. That's all I have to say.'

'And I think it's quite enough,' Magda flared. 'Send me where the dickens you like and see if I care!'

She was so angry at the time that she

193

didn't care, but when she automatically said hello to Anne Gideon in the corridor and was ignored, she began to realize that it might be rather uncomfortable for the next week and it was all so unfair. How dared Jon make her feel it was all like it used to be with them when he knew he was practically engaged to be married? If he'd bought the ring then it was obvious that he was serious. He had never been the type to think of women in any way save as future wives, until last night, that is, when he had obviously simply been reminiscing but, to her cost, making it all appear so real and so true.

When they eventually met in the ward office—Sister being off duty—she was ready for him, therefore.

'Magda,' he said, softly, 'about last night—'

'Don't talk to me about last night,' she flared at him. 'I've never been so embarrassed in my life! I know I'd had too much to drink, but what's your excuse, eh? I suppose I was available and you weren't going to look a gift-horse in the mouth. Was that it?'

He looked subdued. 'I'm sorry if you

194

were embarrassed,' he said. 'I thought it all rather funny.'

'You're the only one who did, then,' she continued to nag. 'I felt a real fool—it was all so—so undignified.'

'You didn't used to mind looking undignified—if that's the word—in such pursuits!'

'I didn't used to a lot of things, but I'm older and wiser, now. I know that men can't be trusted an inch. They ask you to go out for a breath of air and then—then practically rape you—'

'Aren't you being a bit dramatic about it?' he asked coldly.

She knew she had gone too far and made the mistake of going further.

'I was made to appear cheap and dirty. I couldn't bear to look at myself in the mirror this morning. I think you should be ashamed of yourself, and—'

'And I think you should shut up, Magda.' His voice was now blue ice. 'I didn't know you had it in you to be a shrew. You've made everything quite, quite clear and there's no need to refer to the subject again.'

He began to fumble with the kettle switch, without having filled the receptacle.

'Here!' she said, glad of the chance to do something. 'You'll blow us all up. You want a cup of coffee, do you?'

'Yes, please. Hospital coffee is not at all stimulating; thank God! I'm stimulated enough.'

She made the coffee in silence, casting an uneasy glance in his direction occasionally.

'Excuse me, sir,' she said at length, putting them back in their professional rôles, 'but do you know how Nurse Dixon is?'

'We told her friends the usual, as well as can be expected in the circumstances. She's having tests. Didn't they tell you?'

'Actually, I'm—I'm in Coventry.'

'Oh? Why?'

'I was a bit fed up and had a blazing row with them. Sometimes a hospital's like a prep school in its reactions. So she's having tests—for what?'

'Eyesight. Pressure on the brain. She's had a lot of headaches and dizziness lately. She's having bone-marrow extracted on Wednesday.'

'Excuse me, sir,' Magda was almost too agitated to remember not to use his name, 'but all this almost sounds as though you suspect *disseminated sclerosis.*'

'You said that, not I, Staff-nurse. Let's say we hope to eliminate D.S. and then find the real cause of the malady. Don't let's jump our fences, yet, and this conversation never took place.'

'Oh, God! Poor Meg! No, of course it can't be, can it? You have to eliminate it, as you said. I must get back on the ward, back to work and sanity. There's nothing else, is there, sir?'

'No, only work and sanity.' He put his soiled cup in the tiny sink and with a small smile made his exit.

FIFTEEN

Fortunately there was always work, and young Mandy Blake was admitted at two o'clock in renal failure attached to a dialysis machine. There was no room in the Kidney Unit, at present, but the twelve year old was visited by the specialists and poked and prodded and tested in case a transplant should become necessary, and a kind of anger against fate stirred in Magda's bosom as she saw the sick child and wondered what lay between her and the normal good health and high spirits enjoyed by her chums sporting themselves on some hockey or netball pitch. At the best the fifty-fifty chances of transplant surgery, and at the worst...?

'Fancy you getting sick just before Christmas,' Magda said aloud as she helped the child to put on a pretty nightie. 'That was bad management, now wasn't it?'

'I missed the maths exam, though,' the other said, her eyes dancing for a moment above the dark shadows below them, 'I call that good management.'

'You naughty girl!' Magda laughed. 'If I've time I'll set you a few equations myself. No, I don't mean it! Now, what would you like to read? A nice Enid Blyton?'

★ ★ ★ ★

Magda made sure there was nobody else about when she was allowed to visit Meg in the hospital staff sick-bay.

'Thank God it's you!' said the invalid. 'I just don't feel like being jollied along.'

'I hope that's a compliment?' Magda

smiled. 'I know it's boring, but how do you feel?'

'Not bad here. When I go to the toilet I sometimes lose an arm and leg for a moment and think I'm falling. It passes but I feel safe in bed. Not that I'm here for ever. After all the tests I'm to get up and maybe go on light duties. Ah, tea! Join me?'

'Well, this is my tea-break but is it all right?'

'I'll bring another cup and some hot water,' said the elderly nurse.

'I know what they're up to, you know,' Meg suddenly confided.

'Who?'

'The doctors. They think I've got multiple sclerosis. I know, myself, I'm displaying all the classic signs. I once knew a boy in our street who had it.'

'It could be anything at this stage, and you know it,' Magda said, as the nurse reappeared and piled the plate with cakes, knowing at least one of those present would be hungry. 'That's just something the doctors like to eliminate from the start.'

'That's right. Cheer me up. I also know you're not very popular right now.'

'Oh. Who told you?'

'That stupid Winnie Twine couldn't get it out fast enough. Apparently you'd offended her in some way.'

'Today I have managed to offend everyone I know and with bonuses. Should you be speaking to me?'

'I'll risk it. Is it true you were caught in a clinch with Doctor Devon?'

'I was. It may not seem so bad to you when I confide that three years ago we were planning to marry. Oh, never mind what went wrong—we parted in anger, we parted in tears—he's had other affairs and I've been engaged in the meanwhile, but we're not exactly strangers. It won't be happening again, so don't worry.'

'I wouldn't join in the criticism, Magda. Some people simply don't understand how the emotions can create situations. Anyway, my sudden illness has made me realize how good it was to be well. I don't think I'll be worrying much about my love life, or lack of it, if God grants me my health again.'

'I must go. Magda bent to kiss the other. 'I asked Murton to cover an extra five minutes for me and it must be up. Some of us have to work,' and she gave a rueful smile and let herself out of the sick room.

★ ★ ★ ★

The trimmings were going up in the ward. Sister Golightly was hanging a tinselled star above every bed, and displaying shapely legs in black tights so that Jon Devon gave a loud wolf-whistle as he came in.

'Now, none of that nonsense!' Sister said with a smile. 'I'm long past all that kind of thing. Would you carry on, Staff-nurse? I've got them in a red, white and blue sequence, as you see. The blue goes over Mrs. Oliver.'

Magda continued where Sister had left off. She hesitated over the newest arrival on the ward, who was nearest Sister's office, the observation window of which was open. The woman was emerging from a diabetic coma and blinked blearily.

'Now, you're all right, dear,' said Magda. 'We'll take care of you. I'm just going to hang this star over your bed for Christmas. I won't disturb you.'

Up the ladder she could hear Sister's hearty voice in the office.

'Well, I *am* glad she's made her mind up. It's the best thing possible. When's the wedding?'

Magda did not hear the reply, but Sister came again.

'I don't believe in long engagements, either. Well, tell Jane at the party, on Saturday, that although I can't attend I wish her all the very best. We're all joining in to buy an engagement present.'

Magda folded up the ladder quietly and stole away. She had no desire to be an eavesdropper any longer and didn't know how what she had heard unintentionally would affect her when it sank in. Jon and his Jane were announcing their engagement with a party on Saturday, which was Christmas Eve, and if Jane Fulham was holding a party then she was serious. She was not the type to want a crowd around unless the occasion was unique. Shortly afterwards, according to Sister, there was to be a wedding. Great! Happy ever after for some people.

She saw Mandy's hollow eyes regarding her and knew that misery was catching.

'Hello, there!' she said, deliberately brightly. 'I'm just going to hang your presents on the tree, but don't ask me what you're getting because I won't tell.'

★ ★ ★ ★

Fran crept in during the afternoon break and found Magda alone in her room.

'Gosh! But I feel awful!' she exploded.

'Should you be speaking to me?' Magda couldn't resist.

'Well, if for no other reason, the week's up. It's for you to say if you're speaking to us. After all, it *is* Christmas, and I should know. I have a birthday on Christmas Day. I'll be twenty three.'

'Can I buy you a record, or something?' Magda asked.

'Don't you dare! Not after the way you've been treated. I didn't mean to fish. My natal day always gets swallowed up in Christmas spirit.'

'And how's Derek?' Magda asked with interest.

'Derek?' Fran flushed. 'He's going out with that sex-kitten from X-ray, if you must know. I'm intended to be a working girl and I accept it. I'm not like you and Meg, so attractive to the opposite sex that I can pick and choose.'

'I can't exactly pick and choose, either,' said Magda. 'Join the club.'

'So you don't hate us for—?'

'No. I don't hate anybody. I was

annoyed but I've got over it. Ah! the mail! It comes all times at Christmas, doesn't it?'

'I must go and look at mine. I know what all the cards will say. "Have a happy Christmas on your birthday", or "Happy Birthday, Merry Christmas."'

Among Magda's incoming mail was a very nice chiffon scarf, together with a card and letter from Divina Carlyon.

'I shall never forget your kindness and the sympathy between us which made me regard you as my friend,' Divina had written. 'I know you must have nursed hundreds of people in your time, and may have difficulty recalling just one who passed through your hands, but that time at Darfield Park was for me a revelation of both the heights and depths to which people can attain. I am rather sorry that though you did say there was nothing to prevent you in hospital protocol, that you have not been to see me since I let you know I was home from that terrible place in Surrey. In case you have mislaid my address I have written it in large letters above. Do come when you can, you and Doctor Devon both. I would love to see you again. May you have a happy Christmas, my dear. I know it will be busy.

Love, Divina.'

Magda felt quite touched and mean at the same time. She knew there would always be a special feeling between herself and the actress, that their empathy went beyond words. But time was the enemy. There always seemed to be so much to do and so little time for doing it. On her one and only long weekend off duty she had, naturally, gone home, to walk Lassie, the labrador, and tell her parents it was over between herself and Stanley. Now she didn't hesitate. She sought the hall telephone and rang Divina, making an arrangement to call and see her on the following Wednesday afternoon.

All the nurses' rooms looked quite gay as they laid out their Christmas cards from family, friends and—even—patients. It was said about patients that during the time of their incarceration in hospital, a ward became their whole world and those who looked after them more important, temporarily, than the families they had left behind them. Often patients didn't want to leave when they were eventually found to be fit enough to be discharged.

Lonely people, especially with the prospect of returning to empty houses, or flats, would unaccountably have a mild relapse on the evening before they were due to go home. But people once clear of the hospital quickly forgot their attachment to it. Sometimes those who promised to come back and visit did so, but most of them didn't. Coming back as a visitor, watching the nurses busy about their multifarious tasks, and seeing strangers in the beds where one had known friends, put one in the position of being on the outside looking in. Such visitors rarely came again in a purely social sense.

Young Mandy Blake's condition was deteriorating rapidly, and as soon as a kidney machine was available she was to be transferred to the special unit. A transplant was being contemplated if a suitable donor could be found. Both her parents had offered, and been rejected, on medical grounds, and they must have been very worried people, indeed, as they tried to make Christmas wonderful for their only child, who might well never live to see another.

Christmas day dawned with the night-staff touring the wards singing carols, as was usual, wearing their cloaks red side out and carrying lanterns. Victoria yawned awake, those able to wished the others "Merry Christmas" and sank back to await the welcome sound of the early-morning tea-trolley.

All the nurses of Victoria Ward had bought Mandy a present, though patients, like colleagues, were usually exempted from such gestures. She exclaimed, 'Gosh!' and 'Oo, thanks!' as first a record, then a book, a matching woolly hat and scarf and a bottle of perfume were placed on her bed. Sister asked, 'What's all this nonsense, then? Has Santa Claus got past my office undetected? Has he never heard of visiting hours? Just a little something from me,' she added gruffly, and as Mandy struggled she helped her unwrap a pretty little embroidered peasant blouse, having heard the girl say she was getting a new Scottish kilt for Christmas.

Magda couldn't resist looking for signs of last evening's engagement party in Dr. Devon's countenance. He looked as ever, faintly critically at her and then wished a very formal 'Happy Christmas, Staff-nurse!'

'You, too, sir.'

Magda turned to find Winnie Twine tugging at her dress.

'Hello!' she greeted. 'What do *you* want?'

'Well! I like that! I'm sent to help and I'm not wanted.'

'Oh, certainly you're wanted. Here! grab that. Of course your department is shut today and tomorrow, isn't it?'

'Yes. St. Nick's is providing cover for all local casualties whereas our accident unit is remaining open while they have a holiday. Tomorrow I'm to go to Men's Surgical, so make the most of me while you can.'

Even with an extra senior nurse on their strength, there still seemed to be plenty to do. The routine had to go on as usual and there was the seasonal visit from the Mayor and Corporation of the Borough accompanied by Santa Claus, who was, this year, Mr. Carshalton, the neuro-surgeon, with a pillow stuffed up his middle and a deep *basso profundo* of a voice booming out. Every patient received a small gift of either handkerchiefs, toilet accessories or perfume, and then these had to be put away and the wrappings removed, all extra work, before morning drinks could be served.

A small, under-occupied group from the medical staff made their way from ward to ward with a kind of jazz-band composed of a recorder, a tin whistle, a clarinet and a triangle. It was Doctor Orrey on the triangle and he pinged happily.

The patients of Victoria were quite cheered up by this and Magda's heart warmed to all young doctors, brash as they often seemed to be. Staff-nurse Twine was trapped under the mistletoe at the entrance to the ward as the group was departing, and lost her spectacles in a rain of salutes. Everyone was laughing excepting Nurse Murton, who thought such antics rather beneath one.

'The dears!' Sister said fondly at Magda's elbow. 'Oh, I do like Christmas, Staff-nurse! I've forgotten how many I've spent in hospital but every one is as good as the first time. Well, I mustn't stand here sentimentalising. The paper-work has to be kept up to date!'

Magda found herself, with Staff-nurse Twine, folding away the special pink quilts which had been placed on the beds for the Civic dignitaries.

'I say,' confided Winnie, her cheeks

still aglow, 'you don't think the doctors thought I put myself there on purpose, do you?'

'Of course not. It was just your luck to be the one.'

'Do you know, that Doctor Orrey, he really kissed. I can still feel it. George is always a bit respectful, as though I'll break.'

'That's rather nice,' Magda said absently.

'Some people prefer the heavy stuff, the wrestling and the heavy breathing and the passion—'

'When you've finished, Nurses,' said Sister. 'Find out where Nurse Chuong's got to, would you? I will not have my nurses dodging off duty for either a smoke or a sit-down. *I'm* still on my poor feet.'

Nurse Chuong was discovered in the linen-room where she had been trying on a new, red cheongsam.

'Very pretty, Nurse,' said Magda, sternly, 'but you'd better get back to work before Sister finds you. It's nearly dinner-time and you know what that involves on Christmas Day.'

Sir Vivian arrived with the two housemen as the food trolley was delivered. Jon was already there, waiting.

The turkey was revealed under its cover showing one entire side to have been pre-carved.

'A very happy Chwistmas, my dears,' wished the physician heartily, as he forked turkey on the plates while Magda and Sister doled out the roast potatoes and sprouts and Cleo Murton poured gravy over the whole before the three younger nurses acted as waitresses. 'How are they beawing up, Sister?' he asked more quietly, popping a piece of turkey into his mouth and savouring it.

'Oh, very well, Sir Vivian. I really think they'll all do.'

'That's good. Mewwy, mewwy, evewybody! I must go and see my men, now.'

Magda stood in the ward doorway, thankful the procession had left and would not see the amount of food which would be left on the plates. No one who is sick enough to be hospitalized has a very good appetite. She noticed that a few patients were looking at her and smiling.

'Go orn, then!' urged cockney Mrs. Harris. 'Go orn!'

Magda wondered what she was supposed to 'go orn' and do, and turned, only to be caught in a pair of strong, masculine arms and kissed roundly. So this was it. Jon Devon had hung back, seeing her under the mistletoe and knowing how to entertain the bedridden.

'That was purely seasonal,' he whispered, 'but none the less enjoyable. Carry on, Staff-nurse.'

She didn't know whether she wanted to laugh or cry, suddenly. He had engaged himself last night and was kissing her, today, in quite the old way. She wished very much she could hate him, but that would always be impossible, and well she knew it.

★ ★ ★ ★

After Christmas there was suddenly a slump and feelings of depression. Empty beds filled up and the weather turned bitter with a north wind threatening snow. Outside in the world the industrial climate was bitter, too, and there were strikes and go-slows up and down the country. In Darfield Park, a working-class area, many men were idle and the atmosphere was one of gloom.

Nurse Dixon had been sent home for a period of leave. Fran was inconsolable.

'She's got it,' she moaned to Magda. 'They don't know how severely she'll be affected yet, and she's being treated, but I simply can't believe this could happen to her, so lovely, meant to live so fully.'

'It may not be too bad, you know,' Magda felt she had to console the other. 'A young married woman in my village got it and it was practically all over in a month. She's nearly normal again, and has been told she may be in remission for years before she has another attack. From what I hear Meg's coming back to work on P.P.'s. You mustn't depress her, you know, by anticipating the worst.'

'I know. I'm a real wet week. Would you go to the pictures with me Wednesday evening?'

Magda hesitated. She was due to go and see Divina for tea, but if she left about six she should be able to keep Fran company.

'You mean the epic at the Odeon?' she asked. 'I'll meet you outside. It's my half-day off and I'll be doing shopping and the like.'

It was the day of the staff change-over and Magda went on duty to see a cluster of new faces on her ward, all apparently convinced they were not going to like their new appointments.

'Good morning, Staff,' said the third year, a girl named Clements, who introduced himself. 'This is Nurse Augustine,' the West Indian nurse smiled a calypso smile suddenly and closed her mouth again, 'and nurses Waddilove and Stewart. We haven't worked together, before, but we'll try to make a good team.'

'Thank you, Nurse,' Magda said quickly, knowing she had a good ally, here, plain as a suet dumpling as she might be. 'I know it's painful changing duties; I went through it myself a few times at my old hospital. We're an acute medical ward, and nobody's very well here, but there's an opportunity for good nursing experience I hope you'll all appreciate. Now shall we get on with breakfasts? I'll leave you, Nurse Clements, to give everybody a job while I read the night report. Oh! and welcome to Victoria!'

SIXTEEN

Divina admitted her visitor and then curled up on a *chaise-longue,* looking exhausted.

'I felt great in the Nursing Home,' she confided, 'and insisted upon being discharged. But, though I have scarcely a thing to do for myself, it's amazing how even switching on a kettle tires me. How putting on my clothes is suddenly a major operation. Debbie, of course, has to rush off to her classes every morning so I get up to make sure she eats properly. But you don't want to hear my troubles...'

'Of course I do,' Magda insisted. 'What are friends for? I think, perhaps, you're trying to overdo the mothering of Debbie after all these years, rushing round helping *her?* Well, stop that for a start. I'm sure Debbie is capable of seeing to herself and you should lie in until you feel strong enough to cope with your own needs. Walk about in a dressing-gown for the first hour. You have your doctor, of course, and help in the flat?'

'The lot. No expense spared. The doctor comes every day and says nothing but "Hmm!" as he puts his stethoscope away. Adrian arranged with the restaurant up the street to deliver meals and I have a lugubrious little woman comes in to clean, who seems to have lost most of her relatives in particularly grim circumstances and gives me their medical histories, in detail, from first to last.'

Magda smiled.

'Oh, it's so nice to see you, dear! I suppose most of my trouble is loneliness, really. I have too much time to dwell on myself. I have various old friends who write and will, no doubt, be calling on me when they can. Have more tea?'

'I'd love some. I'll fill the pot up. You stay still and make use of me while you can. I thought Debbie's classes wouldn't be starting until some time in January?'

'They don't. But she's having private elocution and deportment lessons in the meantime. She's finding it all very exciting and I hope she doesn't feel, eventually, that the game isn't worth the candle. These are bad times for young people who want to act. When I think of Debbie tagging on with some obscure repertory company, making those awful journeys on Sundays and staying in miserable digs; meeting odd men—' Divina sighed deeply and Magda thought before she spoke again.

'Debbie has her own growing up to do, Miss Carlyon. You can't do that for her. It wouldn't be right if you could. And—and the young usually manage, one way or another.'

'Of course they do. Look at you! So young and yet so in control of her destiny—! I shan't worry any more. There! That's made me feel better.'

A chime ding-donged through the flat.

'I'll answer that,' said Magda, putting down her cup. 'Whom are you expecting?' She opened the front door and gazed uncomprehendingly up into Jon Devon's equally amazed countenance.

'Well, I'll be blowed!' he decided. 'What a coincidence!'

'You'd better come in,' said Magda.

'How nice,' said Divina, 'to see you two together again!'

Magda took another cup from the sideboard and cut another piece of cake, still trying to analyse her feelings on beholding the visitor. There had been a leap of sheer joy within her, quickly quelled as she decided Divina had manoeuvred this.

'I didn't know Staff-nurse was off duty, today,' Jon was saying as he bit into the cake. 'When you 'phoned your invitation, Miss Carlyon, I decided it would give me an opportunity of calling upon an ancient great-aunt of mine, who, independent old soul, lives alone and not one mile away. I've already been to Greenwich, mended a fuse for the old dear and left her a couple of romantic paper-backs, which she loves. You know, the sort where everything comes right in the end.'

'But they never end at the end,' Magda perversely argued. 'You mean they end where a couple come together in either love or marriage. That's really the beginning. They probably scream at each other for the rest of their lives, if the truth was known.'

'How cynical of you, dear!' Divina said.

'I shall not be giving Staff-nurse any romantic paperbacks,' Jon smiled stiffly.

'I think it's great you could both come today,' Divina decided. 'My two favourite people from that great hospital of yours. Neither of you ever reproached me for the horrid publicity I brought in my train. You always made your concern for my condition paramount.'

'Doctor Devon and I only did our job,' Magda said.

'Do you have to call him Doctor Devon off duty, too?'

'I—'

'Magda knows my name', Jon said briskly. 'Of course she doesn't.'

'I have to go, now,' Magda announced. 'May I wash up?'

'Oh,' demurred Divina. 'Must you?'

'I'm going to a film with one of the girls from the hospital.'

'I'll wash up,' Jon Devon offered. 'How are you travelling?'

'By 'bus, of course. There's no problem.' Her eyes warned him to concern himself no more on her account and they must have been particularly communicative for he poured himself a second cup of tea.

'We'll have a gossip, shall we?' he asked Divina. 'I find nothing so relaxing as a good old gossip.'

Magda hurried down the elegant street and turned the corner which brought her to a 'bus-stop with the heath stretching into apparent infinity over the way, where people walked, or played with children or exercised dogs.

219

Magda was aware of a low car drawing up and a young man getting out to help his passenger to alight. It was young Debbie Byngham, prettily dressed, rather over-made-up.

'We'd better say goodbye, here, in case Mama's looking out,' said the girl, and hurled herself into the young man's arms.

Magda had turned away, glad to see that a 'bus was approaching. The girl had gone when she glanced round again and she found herself looking the young man full in the face. It was Eddie Stringer, who had brought all the drama into Divina's life and then, blatantly, tried to feather his nest out of it.

'Oh, no!' was torn from Magda.

Eddie had a puzzled look on his handsome weak countenance as he returned Magda's glance, and then he seemed to recollect her and made as though to speak. She leapt on the 'bus as though escaping from the very mouth of hell.

'Oh, poor Divina!' she thought as the 'bus rattled along. 'If ever she finds out what's going on!'

She was early at the cinema, and practically frozen when Fran joined her.

'Had a good shop?' asked the latter.

'Actually I've been having tea with an ex-patient. You remember the actress?'

'Who could forget that rumpus! Let this be my treat. After all, you came to please me.'

'Don't be silly. We'll go dutch. I don't have to be paid to want your company, Fran. You're my oldest friend at Darfield Park.'

'Bless you! I rang Meg and she was feeling great. She'd only had one symptom all day when she dropped a cup.'

'You see?'

'And it was her mother's best Crown Derby.'

Both girls went laughingly into the auditorium.

Weeks seemed to drag by and yet, anomalously, time sped. The crocuses appeared in the 'garden' in a colourful carpet and the local sparrows made short work of them by pecking out their hearts. No sooner had the groundsman ceased to moan about this than the daffodils came out and danced in the late March breezes. One evening children raided and carried most of them off. It was a constant battle against destructive elements trying to grow anything at Darfield Park Hospital, apart from the tough laurels and privet, but before the wallflowers and tulips should show the gardener prowled most evenings with his crossed fox-terrier-beagle bitch, a female with a renowned mean streak. When Topsy had bitten a visitor and one of the consultants, Barnes was told to leave the animal at home if he valued her life. All the tulip bulbs were dug up one night. Barnes did his expected day's work and gave up after that.

Magda viewed the onset of Spring with mixed feelings. It was pleasant to feel a little warmth in the sun again, though there were always odd odours in the air of Darfield Park as one hopefully gulped it into one's lungs during time allowed for a breather. She had settled down with her new nurses and their different characteristics. Clements was dependable and would make a good Staff-nurse; when Magda discovered she was less adequate on the theoretical side, she gave up her free time to coach the girl. Augustine was sunshine straight from the Caribbean: she filled

Everard's rôle in a way, in that she could cheer the sickest of patients with her continual patter. Waddilove was neat and very serious, not terribly bright but thorough. She took twice as long as anybody else to do the simplest task. On the other hand Stewart was quicksilver and very cocky. Her Scottish voice could be heard jollying Waddilove along; 'Oh, c'm *on!*' she would call. 'I wisht you sassenachs wasna so thick. I didna mean *you*, Staff, it's Waddilove and her whigmaleeries. Turrn the corrner under, you big loon! Honestly, they'll never ha' the likes o' you in a Scottish Hospital.'

Also during this time Magda had her second long weekend off duty and went home. She felt odd, nowadays, at home, however, and found it difficult to be natural with her parents. She felt that she had changed and matured so much in six months that it must be obvious. Her mother tried to discuss the Church bazaar and the W.V.S. but Magda felt such things to be in another dimension. She took Lassie on a long, previously much-loved walk, and merely succeeded in feeling lonely. She visited Huntingdales and was treated as a visitor. Matron even invited her to tea in her office and asked about LONDON—as though it was on another planet. It was with some relief that she caught the 6 o'clock train back on Sunday evening and settled down in a corner to read.

She arrived back at the hospital to hear that young Mandy, who was now in the Kidney Unit, was being tested for her reactions to a possible donor; she heard Meg was holding her own on P.P's and not having too many accidents, that Fran had a new boy-friend in the person of Ikey-Mo Finglestein, and that it was the real thing and why hadn't she noticed him before; and Winnie Twine's contribution was that she really must make up her mind about George one way or another. This was now the familiarity and she looked on Darfield Park Hospital as her new home.

Jon Devon's visits to the ward were brusque and business-like and when Magda offered, sometimes unhappily, to make him refreshment after his rounds, especially on days when Sister was not on duty, he was more likely to refuse than not, and if he accepted they talked of patients or the weather or Mandy, whether she would lead a life independent of machines ever again.

There were odd moments, however, when, almost against their wills, eyes would meet and ricochet away as though the impact was physically painful. Magda imagined that this was all in her mind, as she was the hurt one and Jon had his Jane, which must be a great consolation to him. She never ceased to be physically aware of him and even considered handing in her notice and going to work elsewhere, but always she convinced herself that it would get better and she would get over him all over again, but as April stepped in on March's coat-tails, which had gone out like a lion, weeping and shining most typically, she knew that she would never settle for second best, again, in the love stakes. It was all or nothing, and in her case she sought compensations, not new conquests.

Not only young men's fancies turned to thoughts of love at this season; several nurses announced their engagements and carried their precious rings around in the breast pockets of their uniforms when on duty. The S.N.O. advised the more senior to finish their training before contemplating marriage, so that they could come back as young matrons to further their careers and family incomes.

On this early April day Magda was late to midday meal and would have been content to sit in the nearest vacant place, but Fran Briscoe called urgently so as not to be denied.

'Magda! There's room here. Come on!'

Magda sat between male-nurse Finglestein and Elsie Lyons and looked at the unappetising bowl of powdery soup set in front of her.

'Don't worry,' said Fran, passing the bread, 'there's worse to come. It's fish pie. When anything arrives in the form of a pie one can't help but wonder what has gone into it. Sorry, old thing, I didn't mean to put you off!'

'I think my hunger may overcome my repugnance. One must always remember that Dietitians are working on our behalf. I'm sure all our calories and vitamins are in there somewhere.'

'We wondered,' said Meg, who was across from her, apparently her own lovely self apart from a weakness in her right hand. She ate with the fork in her left, 'if you would care to contribute to a wedding present?'

'Well, of course!' Magda said promptly. 'Who's getting married?'

'Apparently it's all supposed to be rather hush-hush, but you know there are ways and means of finding things out?'

'So I do!'

'It seems that Sister Fulham has stated her intention to the S.N.O. of marrying very quietly on the Saturday before Easter.'

Magda did not even choke, though she thought that one or two of those present might expect her to do so.

'So how much is everybody giving?' she asked calmly.

'That's up to the individual,' said Elsie Lyons. 'As I work with Sister Fulham I'm giving her a present on my own. But she's so nice and popular, as *he* is, so we thought a present from the staff would be a gesture.'

'I agree,' said Magda, felt in her pocket for her purse and pulled out a pound note. 'Is that in order?'

'I say, that's jolly generous of you! Thanks.'

'Of course while it's hush-hush,' Fran

commented, 'we can't congratulate them openly. They'll ask how we came to hear and we can hardly say the news was passed on by the S.N.O's personal maid, who leaked it to Charlie, the porter, after the old girl had invited Sister to dine with her, now can we? Doctor Devon's a very lucky man,' and she tried to avoid looking at Magda as she said it whereas Meg tried to capture her gaze, looking understandingly sympathetic.

'I heard Sir Vivian congratulating Doctor Devon in the corridor outside Alexandra,' contributed Anne Gideon. 'I was making drinks in the kitchen. He said "By the way, congratulations, my boy! I just heard! Well done!" I didn't know what it was all about at the time, but now one can put two and two together.'

Magda thought the fish-pie was going to make her sick, and it *would* be the pie, though nobody would believe it. She breathed deeply and determined to empty her plate.

'Well, it's nice to talk about other people's romances,' said Elsie Lyons. 'There's not much going on in our ranks.'

'Speak for yourself,' said Fran, giving

her 'Ikey' a quick cuddle.

'And I'm thinking of taking the plunge again,' said Winnie.

There were noisy sounds of utter disbelief.

'Scoff as you may,' Winnie said loudly. 'I'll become a bride this year or bust. How about you, Magda? I know Doctor Gregory's keen on you.'

'No speculation, please!' begged Magda. 'I'm not rising to that one. I hope you'll all ask me to your weddings. That's the next best thing.'

She could afford to allow her innermost feelings to surface as she returned to the ward for the comparative peace of afternoon duty. It seemed there was a hurt within her so deep that it would never find ease. Her very spirit seemed to be frozen in the middle of a scream against the unkindness of fate. Of course one could not always believe rumour, but this was smoke from the very heart of a fire which could not be ignored. She wondered if—in their peculiar circumstances—he would tell her the news personally. This would not assuage her distress one iota but it would confirm that he still respected her for what she had meant to his past.

SEVENTEEN

He came accompanying an emergency admission in cardiac failure. Casualty had 'phoned the ward and Magda had the bed near the door curtained off and ready. Nurse Stewart had filled a couple of hot water bottles and brought an extra blanket, as instructed, and then made herself scarce. She was in the sluice writing a letter home to her family in Scotland, telling them how much she was earning and learning and that she wasn't standing any nonsense from anybody, which had been her eldest brother's advice, who had also trained in sassenach country and was now a practising doctor in Edinburgh.

Jon required Magda to help him set up a saline drip as the woman in the bed was badly dehydrated and needed fluid urgently. They worked quickly and efficiently and eventually the patient stirred and sighed.

'Another one to us, I think,' Jon decided, seeking the pulse. 'Come on, Mrs. Carson!

Let's see what colour eyes you've got.' He injected her with coramine as he spoke.

The woman did eventually open her eyes and said, 'Oh, my God! I feel so weak.'

'You'll be O.K. now,' Jon said. 'If I were you I'd go back to sleep. Nothing to worry about.'

'Thanks, Doctor.'

Magda asked, dubiously, as they left the cubicle, 'I don't suppose you'd like a cup of coffee?'

'No, thanks.' He frowned for a moment. 'But a cup of tea, yes. Can you manage that?'

'I do believe Sister has some tea-bags.' She led the way into Sister's office and he peered through the glass window which looked into the ward.

'I think our Mrs. Carson is asleep already with the good Nurse Clements to keep her company. These rheumatic-damaged hearts! I wonder if their owners know how near the brink they go at such times? It could be our dear Divina all over again, couldn't it?'

'I don't suppose Mrs. Carson will bring quite the same excitement to the ward, sir.'

The kettle boiled and switched itself off.

Magda poured water over a tea-bag in Sister's tiny, china pot and allowed the brew to infuse with help from a stir of the spoon.

'I believe congratulations are in order?' she heard herself asking cheerfully.

Jon Devon stared as she poured his cup of tea with a slightly unsteady hand.

'How on earth did you hear about that?' he countered.

'Oh—' she shrugged '—are there any secrets for long in this place?

'Well, I'm jiggered! I thought only a handful knew. Anyhow, thanks!'

'I hope you'll be very happy,' she proclaimed from the depths of her own, personal grieving.

'Oh, I'm sure I will be when I get used to the idea. It hasn't quite registered yet. It's quite a responsibility, really.'

'But one you welcome? You must welcome it?'

'Yes, of course. Thanks, Magda.' He set down his empty cup and this time looked out of the main window towards the new medical wing, where the workmen had stopped yet once again for a cuppa. It surprised him to think of the wing being anywhere near finished by the autumn, when a royal duchess had consented to perform the opening ceremony.

'How are things with you?' he asked.

She had been washing the cup, emptying the pot. 'Oh, fine. Fine, thanks.' I'm saying everything twice like a parrot, she thought to herself.

He turned and looked at her directly.

'I suppose you're still as determined as ever to stay in your job?'

'Of course I am. I have no reason for dropping it.'

'Yes. I see. Thanks for the tea.'

Perhaps a fellow feeling of disturbance made Magda the more kind in that she consented to go out with Winnie Twinc one evening. It had been raining and was cool so they took a five-penny 'bus ride to the shops and just strolled round.

'I say, Magda, you don't think George will do it again, do you?'

'Do what, Winnie?' as if she didn't know!

'Not turn up at the wedding. I couldn't bear it a second time. I would want to die. Really I should have stood firm and not looked at him again, but I can't seem to stop thinking about him. I dream about him, I think I see him when I'm out;

many's the time I've almost touched a perfect stranger on the shoulder because he looked like George from behind, or because he was wearing a jacket like George's. I'll be getting myself run in for—for soliciting, or something. I'm obsessed with George, still, and I know it's not healthy. He wants us to marry at Whitsun, but I don't know. I don't really know.'

'You're obviously made for each other,' said Magda. 'At the dance he told me you'd have been married within a week of the *débacle* if your mother hadn't talked you out of it. He says you're too easily influenced by other people.'

'Well, my mum appealed to my pride, what was left of it. "He let you down," she said, "and we had to pay for the miserable reception without any wedding. Your dad and me didn't know where to put ourselves." Neither did I, Magda, neither did I.'

'Of course you have your pride, but is that enough? Obviously not, or you wouldn't still be dreaming of George. Other bridegrooms have caught cold feet before this, and many have married their girls later. It's something so personally psychological it's difficult to explain or understand. I'm sorry to keep on, Winnie, but I think the next step is up to you, and without advice from your mother. I adore my own mother, but parents can't live our lives for us. We have to make important decisions for ourselves.'

'Well, thanks for listening, anyway, Magda. I suppose I'll think seriously about Whitsun, but I'll be glad when it's safely over, if you understand.'

'Of course I do. We'd better get back, eh? I never seem to get enough sleep. I even envy the patients lying in bed sometimes.'

★ ★ ★ ★

Easter crept inexorably nearer, though it was late that year. Magda marked off every day on her pocket calendar and heard at the meal-table that Sister Fulham had been amazed and almost tearful to receive the staff's gift of a very nice coffee-service.

'Oh! you naughty things!' she had told Staff-nurse Lyons. 'I thought we were keeping our secret so well. Of course a few officials had to be told, but—' and then she had laughed and cried at the same time.

'I'm invited to the reception after the wedding,' said Elsie Lyons. 'Sister said she hadn't any more official cards, as they'd expected only a quiet family do, but that I must go round to the flat for a drink and a piece of cake.'

On Good Friday Magda found time, and the urge, to attend Church. She sat from two until three o'clock putting herself in the mood of the sadness of the world, and then concluding that rejoicing must surely come later. She emerged from the building comforted and calm, hoping for lovely weather on the morrow for the happy couple, and having said a prayer for their welfare.

She was to work Saturday morning and then was free for the next thirty-six hours. She had thought about going home but fancied she might be miserable company for her parents and so decided against it. So far she had no plans of how she would spend her time off. She was thinking in rather desperate terms of running out of the hospital at one o'clock and not stopping until she fell down exhausted, maybe at Watford Junction if she ran up the M.1.

'No pedestrians allowed,' she smiled

grimly, so that Nurse Clements asked, 'Pardon, Staff?'

'Overwork, Nurse,' Magda told her. 'I was just rambling on to myself.'

She continued to work diligently and was surprised to see Jon Devon come in for a brief round. She had expected him to be free on his wedding day from the cares of the ward.

'We'll miss Doctor Devon,' Sister said later.

Magda agreed almost too readily.

'But our loss is another's gain,' said Sister Golightly. 'He has to seize his opportunities. He's a brilliant diagnostician and Sir Vivian was right behind his decision all the way.'

Magda asked, 'Are we losing Doctor Devon for good, then, Sister?'

The other put a hand quickly to her lips and then said, 'Come and have a coffee in my office, Staff-nurse. Me and my big mouth!' When they were alone she said, 'I wasn't supposed to say anything. Doctor Devon would hate goodbyes. Please don't let this go any further, dear. Forget what I said.'

'I didn't know he was leaving Darfield Park for good,' Magda repeated, dully.

'Well, I've asked you to forget it, Staff-nurse. Brew up, there's a good girl.'

Magda's thoughts were rioting. She had expected Jon to go away on honeymoon and then return to his job. Even that thought had been a sort of consolation.

'Now that you've told me so much, Sister, could you tell me where Doctor Devon's talents will be used in future?'

'Well, knowing it won't go any further I think I can drop a little hint. It's one of the big ones.'

'The Middlesex?' Magda asked. 'Guy's?' as Sister smiled and shook her head. She named another famous hospital and the other nodded.

'Well, I'm glad he's made the top. He really is wasted at Darfield Park.'

They stopped chatting and looked up in amazement as the object of their discussion knocked on the door and entered. He looked unfamiliar in a tail-suit of light grey, wore a cravat and a carnation in his button-hole and rather self-consciously carried a grey top hat.

'I'm just off,' he announced.

'You look lovely,' Sister Golightly said happily, 'and you've got a glorious day for it.'

Somehow Magda's eyes seemed to have sunk into her head and were burning her brain.

'If anyone comes to relieve they'll need these,' he put a set of keys on the table which Sister promptly locked in her desk drawer.

Magda found herself saying 'Good luck!' without adding sir.

'Thanks. I'll need it,' and he was gone.

'Now that,' said Sister, 'is what I call a very happy ending to an affair which has had us all guessing for some time. We all wanted Jane Fulham to find happiness again, and now she has.'

Magda returned to the ward to fulfil her last duties of the morning and then thankfully went off duty. She couldn't bear to see her friends at the meal table today, of all days, so she went to the canteen and ordered a round of sandwiches and a pot of tea.

She supposed the wedding would be over, now, and there would be the reception, the speeches, the exchange of tender glances as Jon referred to 'My wife and myself,' and the laughter, the toasts, the getting changed and the going away just to be together. Two people happily made one as nature intended.

'Why do I still feel about him so keenly?' Magda asked herself desperately. 'He's forgotten me. Why can't *I* forget *him?* But not to see him again, either! That's an added blow. I honestly don't think I can take it.'

A voice asked, 'Have I caught you at a bad moment, Staff-nurse?'

Magda looked up dully into the concerned countenance of Doctor Nat Gregory. She had not been talking aloud, but her undisturbed tray of food and three screwed up napkins spoke volumes.

'I beg your pardon?' she asked.

'May I join you? Or would you rather be alone?'

'Oh, do join me, Doctor. I'm not very good company.'

'I thought maybe you had a headache, or something.'

'It's "or something",' she told him. 'One of those days when you wish you had a gas-oven.'

'Oh, Staff-nurse! You *must* be blue. Are you off duty?'

'Until Monday morning. I can be blue all that time if I wish to indulge.'

'I have a better suggestion to make if

you're interested. *I'm* free, too. Go out with me and I'll try to make you feel better.'

Magda looked with those deep hollow eyes into Nat Gregory's red-gold ones. At the Founder's Day dance he had said they might meet again one day, a polite comment which left them free to take up the option in the future if so inclined. The other nurses said he was keen on her. Maybe he looked at her a little overlong at times, but he was not a Doctor Orrey to count his conquests by the dozen and he had made no obvious advances to her until this moment.

Now she said, 'I would take you up on that, Doctor, so long as you understand I have nothing to offer you but my dubious companionship. I am not remotely interested in you as a man, nor other men. I don't wish to be rude but I'm not looking for the usual distractions between members of the opposite sex. You could enjoy your off-duty in so many other ways.'

'Well, that's very frank of you, Staff-nurse—'

'The name's Magda.'

'Magda, then. You look as if you need caring for. Would you accept my offer of escort and friendship? I got your original message loud and clear. I'm Nat, by the way.'

'Well, Nat, I do feel a bit rudderless today. I would appreciate being cared for. What exactly do I do?'

'You'll want to change out of uniform?' Magda nodded. 'I'll be waiting for you outside the Home in fifteen minutes. Will that be enough?'

'I'll be ready. Oh, and thanks, Nat! You could well be my angel in disguise.'

'My God! I didn't know I was so good at disguises.'

She reappeared with a small suitcase and a too-bright smile. 'I don't know about you, Nat, but I'm not coming home tonight. I have a sleeping-out pass.'

He did not comment only to say, 'As you wish. I don't need one. I have to be back to be on call Sunday evening if that's all right with you.'

'That's fine.'

'We've just got to call in at my place. I need pyjamas and toothbrush.'

She never recognised cars as some girls do, but this was new and low-slung and orange in colour and comfortable. It went Harumph! and Grmm! once it was in gear and shot far too fast out of the hospital grounds, down the Kent road and then into a little cul-de-sac of chi-chi houses.

'I share with Carter and Dalgliesh,' Nat explained, 'but they're grinding away today. Come on in for a drink while I get ready.'

The maisonette would have made two women very happy, but three young men had created pandemonium therein. Books were everywhere, together with records and cassettes. From the kitchen washing-up overflowed.

'Our Mrs. Mopp hasn't been in,' fretted Nat. 'Can you find a seat? Would you like sherry or something stronger?'

'Oh, sherry's fine, thanks.'

With a glass in her hand she saw Nat, in a bedroom whose door would not close for things hanging on it, shoving pyjamas and Y-fronts into a holdall. With any other man these would have appeared to be the preliminaries to a dirty weekend, but Magda had delivered herself up in all innocence to this man and knew in her heart whatever plans he had for her were innocent. Once the car was Harumphing and Grumphing once more she asked, 'Where are we going, Nat?'

'I thought—Brighton.'

'Oh. That sounds original.'

'Have you ever been?'

'No.'

'Well, it's nice. The run's pleasant and one can do things or not when one gets there. There's always the beach and we can play ducks and drakes on the tide.'

'It's a long time since I played that. I hadn't the patience to look for the flattest stones and my brother always beat me.'

'I shall try to beat you, too.'

It was better being cared for by a friend than running up the M.1., she decided. She was beginning to feel just a little bit better about everything and realizing that what was done could not be undone. It was a gorgeous day, and not only for weddings. The downs were dressed overall for Spring and on the high ground in folds were carpets of primroses.

Nat knew Brighton well, and took her to a tea-room run by maiden sisters who still produced the real thing, Earl Grey in china cups and gooseberry jam on brown and white bread cut thin, scones with cream and a home-made fruit cake.

They then went to the 'George Hotel' to get rid of their bags and park the car.

'Two singles, please,' Nat ordered at the reception desk, 'for one night.'

'Connecting rooms, sir?'

'Good gracious, no! The lady would like one with bath but a shower will do for me.'

The receptionist looked at Magda and wondered what was amiss with the young buck or, rather, how they were going to wangle it despite all this casualness of approach.

'Now for the ducks and drakes before dark,' Nat said quite excitedly, no doubt recollecting his little boy days. 'Then I'm going to treat you to a seven course dinner with champagne. Is it all right up to now?'

'Oh, Nat!' she squeezed his arm chummily. 'You are really taking care of me and I honestly didn't know how I was going to get through this day. Here it is nearly over.'

'Not nearly,' he denied, 'but it's not at all bad being a friend. Not nearly as bad as I feared.'

Magda had similar sentiments as she prepared to bath before getting into bed. She had been hauled along a mile of beach, then fed like a pig for market and surfeited with Champagne until she caught the giggles. As though that wasn't enough Nat suggested a walk round the town and by this time it was so late, and she was so tired, that she knew she would be incapable of thinking of anything but sleep.

The suspicious receptionist had passed on his thoughts to the night porter, who kept a strict eye on rooms nine and fourteen, but nothing happened so far as he could tell, unless it went on by remote control nowadays.

EIGHTEEN

Other people had their own fish to fry on this same evening, who are connected with this history.

Fran came flying out of the Nurses' home, her coat buttons undone, and flung herself upon the good-looking dark young man with the slightly prominent nose of his race.

'Hello, Ikey-Mo,' she greeted rapturously, pouting for a kiss.

'Hello, Ginger!'

Fran stopped in her tracks, lowering her hands from his shoulders.

'Why did you call me that? Don't you like red hair all of a sudden?'

'I love it. Especially on you, pet.'

'My schooldays were ruined by people calling me Ginger, I'd have you know. I thought I'd outgrown that.'

'I thought I'd outgrown being called Ikey-Mo. The name's Daniel.'

'Sorry, Dan.' She grinned at him suddenly and offered to kiss and make up. 'I'm so nervous of meeting your parents. Won't they resent the fact that I'm not Jewish?'

'They might, but they know their Dan will have his way whatever they resent. They won't be rude, or anything. You'll like my dad. He's a real East-Ender born and bred and will deal in anything. He'll probably offer to get you a fur coat at a tenth of the price, or something.'

'And your Mother?'

'She can be funny with girls I bring home.'

'How many have you taken home, then, Ikey—I mean, Dan?'

'I'm not a poof you know. I take girls

home if I like 'em.'

'So I'm just one of many? Nothing special?'

'You could be very special if you'd stop needling me for five minutes. Oh, Fran, don't let's get on edge with each other or the parents will sense it and think we're not sure of ourselves. I want to introduce you as the girl I intend to marry. Now's the time to back out if you're not sure, so think about it.'

'I've thought about it for a week. But I can't help feeling nervous. You'll stay close to me, Dan, won't you?'

They were soon in Hackney and changing to a local 'bus. The street where Dan lived was long with area gardens and bow-windowed houses. In some of the windows the seven candles of the Jewish sabbath were burning, and Fran panicked when she saw that such candles burned behind the window where Dan stopped. She found herself running, running away, until Dan's feet pounded up to her and she was seized and shaken.

'You—you said—' gasped Fran— '—you said they weren't orthodox. You said—'

'Look, honey, they're not. That's my mum's ploy to try you. The acid test.

You're a gentile entering a Jewish household. Stand up and face it. You'll probably never see the candles lit again in our house in a lifetime, unless there's a blackout?'

Fran allowed herself to be led back to the house and gripped Dan's hand tightly.

'Here we go!' he said encouragingly, and nonchalantly opened the door to lead her into his home.

* * * *

Meg had had a pretty good day but was tired and wanted only to sit in her room for awhile and then get into bed. She tired easily. Sister on P.P's would say, 'Well done, Staff-nurse,' when she dropped something, 'but you mustn't overdo things. Sit in my office for half an hour. If you feel like filling in a few charts I'd be obliged.'

It was not easy to write, but she persevered and was beginning to practice with her left hand in her own time.

Doctor Matthews, the consultant neurologist, had been most encouraging. He had given her tablets which cleared up the headaches in no time.

'Oh, you may get away fairly lightly,' he had told her during her last examination. 'The arm is weak and may remain so. You may have some trouble with your leg. You don't drive, do you? Good! We may be able to control the whole thing with drugs so that you lead a fairly normal life. Have you a boy friend? Not seriously? A girl like you? What are they thinking of! Anyway, providing you continue to stabilize there's no reason why you shouldn't marry and have a family eventually. We're always a bit in the dark with this joker but I'm beginning to hope you're going to be one of the lucky ones, my dear. Keep in good spirits. There's no need to come and see me again unless you have any new and alarming symptoms.'

Meg yawned and decided to slip into bed and read for an hour or so. She had the latest Jean Plaidy out of the hospital library and found reading such books was an easy and entertaining way of learning about history. None of those boring dates one had had to recite at school and all the drama and romance somehow potted. As her right hand tired holding the book she automatically changed over to her left, something she was now learning to do without thinking. She turned over the better to see, growing a little impatient as her right foot caught in the bedclothes and was slow to release itself. She felt a rising of impatience in her chest and then deliberately made herself calm down: should she ever feel agitated she had only to ask Home-Sister for a Valium tablet, but she did not relish becoming a drug addict. She looked back at the page she was reading, realizing she had already read it once without registering. Now it developed an awful fascination for her, for every word was duplicated, slightly above and to the right. It must be a printer's error! She turned a page, and that was the same so she whipped pages back she knew to be all right only they weren't, the blurring duplication was everywhere. She put the book down and looked at the bedside light; it had a paler ghost hovering above it. There were two dressing tables, two photographs of her parents on them and two chairs. In another direction there were four hooks behind the door whereas before there were only two.

She shook her head, closing her eyes and opening them again warily. Nothing had changed. The room was a mass of distortions as tears gathered in her eyes. She got out of bed and pulled on one of the two dressing-gowns from behind the door; the second mysteriously faded. She opened her door and ran down the corridor calling, 'Fran! Fran!'

Her friend was not in, however, nor was Magda, nor Anne, nor anyone of her familiars. Home-Sister hauled her into her private room knowing by instinct that something terrible was amiss; when eventually she had stumbled downstairs.

'I'm seeing double, Sister. I can see two of you. Would you call that a—a new and alarming symptom?'

Sister Friar knew from experience that comfort and reassurance are always the best medicines.

'It's a symptom, Staff-nurse. Tomorrow you'll probably be as right as rain again. Now I see you're all ready for bed so I'm going to put you in my spare room, then you'll know I'm right here. You're to take a couple of mogodons. Oh, yes, I have the authority to insist. That's right. Let me tuck you in. I'll just make a nice cup of cocoa and then it's ten solid hours for you, do you hear?'

Meg heard. A whimper left her lips,

but when Sister returned with the drink and the tablets she appeared calm and obediently allowed herself to be drugged into a deep and oppressed sleep.

★ ★ ★ ★

Winnie Twine took a hot chipped potato from the packet George held out to her.

'Hm! These are good. What was the name of that boat, again?'

'The "Cutty Sark", and she's not a boat she's a ship. A Clipper.'

'Oh, George, you know so much I don't know what you see in poor ignorant me!'

'See in you? I love you. Added to that you're a damned good nurse.'

'Do you think I'm pretty?'

'Do you think I'm handsome?'

They looked at each other in the lights from the Greenwich Naval College, outside which they had arrived, and collapsed into laughter.

'No. We're not much cop where looks are concerned, are we? I pity our kids if we have any. That's if we get married, of course.'

'What do you mean "if"? I thought at last it was all settled. I've even given in about that tribe of Liverpudlians you want to invite.'

'Well, I have a lot of relations. I can't help that. They were all in at my shame so I want them to witness my triumph. I would naturally like to ask a few personal friends, too. I've taken a lot of ragging from the girls I know at the hospital and I don't think they'll ever believe it's done unless they see it. If you agree we'll go ahead and I'll order the cards next time I'm out.'

'Winnie,' he pulled her to face him and his plain, bespectacled face looking into her plain bespectacled face was serious. 'I have one ever-abiding doubt about us. Please put my mind at rest once and for all. Do you just want a wedding or do you really want me? I mean, after it's over, and your relations have gone back to Slough and Birmingham and Liverpool, will I be enough or will there be an eternal sense of disappointment in your heart? I don't think I'm a great lover. I mean I've never tried. I—'

'George,' she said softly, 'I'm sure you'll be a smashing lover. If you've never tried, how do you know? You're going to have to teach me a thing or two because I've never done anything like that, either. I really want the wedding to be over so we can adventure a little together. Of course, being a nurse, I know all about it in theory but they say—the other girls, I mean—that it's all so wonderful you can't even describe it. Dear George! I'll come home from work and love washing your shirts and mending your socks and cooking your suppers, and every time anybody calls Mrs. Whale I'll grow two extra inches.'

A few naval cadets disturbed the embrace which followed, making kissing noises and whistling derisively.

'Honestly!' George said pettishly. 'There's nowhere in the whole of London for sweethearts to be at peace. Snotty little kids! They'll be dirty sailors this time next year.'

'Come on, George,' said Winnie, quite happily. 'You'd better get me back to the hospital or we'll be forgetting how we always said we would wait until after we were married for you know what!'

★ ★ ★ ★

Sunday it rained.
Magda awoke about nine and was

relieved that the worst hours of her ordeal were well and truly over.

'After all, I've been through it before,' she told herself, 'So I have had some practice.'

There was a knock on her door and a maid arrived at her invitation.

'I have to give you this, Miss.' "This" was a cup of steaming tea with two biscuits in the saucer. 'The gentleman along the passage wants to know if you're going down to breakfast or would you prefer it in your room? But we only do continentals on room-service.'

Magda remembered Nat in all this adventure with a slight acknowledgement of shame. He had given his all in helping her through a crisis and received nothing in return. If only one could fall in love with the people who were so right for one in every way!

'Tell Doctor Gregory I'll see him in the dining-room,' she instructed.

'Ooh! Is he a doctor? He looks so young.' The maid twittered off on bunion-distorted feet and Magda drank the tea and looked ruefully at the rain-spattered windows beyond which the gulls made a peculiarly wet-day protest by sitting on every roof and chimney-pot and ruffling their feathers. There was no sign of a break in the clouds as she dressed after a quick, cool bath, but it was still April and the sun could well be shining by afternoon.

'So what do we do?' she asked Nat, when by eleven o'clock there was no let-up in the weather. 'We can't go to Hastings on such a day, can we? It wouldn't be fair on the place. It was probably raining on the day King Harold got the arrow through his eye, otherwise he might have seen it coming.'

'Would you object if we went back? We can stop for lunch on the way.'

'Not at all. I think that's a very good idea. I'll just get my things together.'

She found Nat paying both bills and was prepared to protest.

'I'm not a pauper,' she told him. 'I can pay my way.'

'Look, Magda,' he drew her out of the receptionist's hearing, 'I offered to take care of you, didn't I? That I chose to do it in Brighton was not of your choosing, but mine. Now I have respected your original veto and still enjoyed your company. I would like you to respect my pride. *I* pay when I take a girl out, no matter what we do. O.K.?'

She ceased to protest and he brought the car to the hotel door to collect her, his shoulders wet from his dash to the car-park. They had neither of them thought to bring macs.

"Grumph," as she now called the car, made a great show of climbing the roads leading to the Downs. Magda saw cattle huddled in hollows and under the scrubby trees.

'That's a bad sign,' her country upbringing had taught her. 'When they do that it's going to rain for the foreseeable future.'

They decided to lunch at Hayward's Heath, and took their time over the meal. Magda had *duc à l'orange* and Nat hake in a cream sauce.

'We should be back in just over an hour if there's not much traffic,' Nat philosophized, so at three-thirty "Grumph" was off again. Within the hour they were at East Grinstead when Nat said, 'I'm sorry, but I feel awful. I've got gut-rot, or something. I must stop at a public lavatory.'

He came out, getting wet, but laughing again. 'That's better,' he decided. 'Gosh! but I needed that.'

Crawling towards Cattershaw they had

had to stop five times, sometimes when there was nothing more private than a hedge. As Magda saw her companion coming towards her, soaked to the skin and looking pale and grey, she helped him into the passenger-seat and took over.

'Look, Nat! *I* can drive. I'll go slowly but we're going to find a doctor or a hospital in Cattershaw. You've obviously got food poisoning and the sooner the source is traced the better.'

The Military Hospital personnel were most co-operative when Magda got past the guards at the gate. Nat wasn't up to much argument and was helped inside while Magda sat in reception and watched army nurses doing her job yet looking so different in their smart uniforms.

'Hello!' an M.O. came to greet her. 'We're going to keep your friend overnight and if he's not O.K. in the morning we must transfer him to the civilian hospital in the town. Meanwhile we've let the authorities both in Hayward's Heath and Brighton know where you stayed and ate. They're going to investigate.'

'Nat is going to be all right, isn't he?' Magda asked in alarm.

'Oh, my dear, you came to the right

place. We're always poisoning ourselves in barracks. He'll be fine anon, as they say.'

'He's due on call at seven in *our* hospital.'

'Then they'll have to find someone else, won't they? Do feel free to use our 'phone. The corporal on the switchboard, there, will get your number.'

'I have to be on duty in the morning and what about the car?'

'I should take it and scuttle off. When our friend is well enough we'll get him back somehow. I'll explain you've gone. He couldn't care less, anyway, at the moment.'

Magda rang up Darfield Park Hospital and found herself telling the Chief Hospital Administrator what had happened. He told her not to worry, asked if she had any similar symptoms and invited her to call and see him as soon as she got back.

Thus, at a little before eight o'clock, with the rain easing but still determinedly falling, she told her story to Doctor Fawley, who now worked in an administrative rôle only.

'So far there have been no complaints of a similar nature from either place, but I, personally, suspect that cream sauce.

One unhygenic finger in contact with one spoonful could have laid our poor chap low. I think you did very well, Staff-nurse, taking over the driving and finding a hospital. If he'd passed out at the wheel it could have been nasty. It's been a rotten holiday Sunday so the roads have been quiet, at least.'

'Of course!' Magda said in a tone of wonderment. 'It's Easter Sunday, isn't it? I'd forgotten that.'

'In the course of the pursuits of youth, Staff-nurse, one can forget much. I rang up the S.M.O. Cattershaw, by the way, a few minutes ago, and our hero is taking liquids. I should go and get your supper, now, before they scoff the lot. Sunday supper makes up, usually, for a multitude of catering sins.'

Because the good doctor had gone on to other subjects, Magda did not see fit to take him up on that 'pursuits of youth' crack. Nobody would believe her if she told the simple truth of the matter, so why should she bother? She had handed the car-keys to Doctor Dalgliesh and told him what had happened and he had given her some very odd looks, too, while expressing sympathy for his colleague.

★ ★ ★ ★

There was no avoiding Fran on this evening. She set herself squarely in front of Magda and said, brightly, 'Hello, stranger! Where've you been?'

'Here and there,' Magda replied. 'I was officially off-duty so I don't have to account to anyone.'

'I take your point. Forgive me if I was so chuffed with my newly-engaged status that I dared to want to confide in a chum about it.'

'Oh, congratulations!' Magda said, and quickly reached and kissed the other.

'Oh! no need to be sloppy,' Fran said happily. 'You'll be addressing my mail to Mrs. D. Finglestein after August. My God! What a name! Why couldn't he have been called Smith?'

'What's in a name?' smiled Magda, accepting a bowl of tomato soup.

'Exactly. Meg had a funny turn with her eyes. She has to see the neurologist again, tomorrow, but so far, today, she's been O.K.'

'Gosh!' Magda exclaimed. 'I turn my back for five minutes and it's like reading the News of the World when I get back!'

'Anyhow, how was Brighton? *Do* have the roast pork, it's good.'

'I will, thanks. I know I shouldn't ask, but how did you know I'd gone to Brighton?'

'Well, why shouldn't you, old thing? Being a newly-engaged lady I'm broad-minded all of a sudden. Actually I heard because Carrie Moore's been wangling like mad for a date with our sexy Doctor Orrey, and she was told an hour ago to abandon hope for tonight. Dear Ken has been told to stand by on call in Doctor Gregory's place. Ken was heard to proclaim that people enjoying dirty weekends in Brighton should take all the usual precautions, including watching what they damned well ate. He had one or two things to say about you, too, such as you keeping up a pose where butter wouldn't melt in your mouth until you felt the itch. He said he was surprised at Nat Gregory, who was inclined to be critical of other people, meaning him.'

Magda said, 'I'll have a word with Doctor Orrey, defaming two characters. It was *not* a dirty weekend and as my friend I expect you to believe me, at least. O.K.?'

'If you say so,' Fran shrugged. 'O.K.'

'Well Nat Gregory is a wonderful friend and I won't have a word said against him.'

'That's the spirit. I'm glad you two finally got together, in the nicest way, of course. He's a quiet lad and has had his eye on you for quite some time. Have you—er—finished? We're the last two in the dining-room. Let's go up to your room and I'll make us coffee up there.'

Magda wondered at Fran's predilection for her company when the sitting-room was full and the T.V. going full blast showing an old film. She sat in her room brushing her hair, which was still damp from a couple of soakings she had suffered during the day, while Fran was busy in Kitty's small kitchen making the coffee. She appeared with two beakers on a tin tray.

'Rapunzel, Rapunzel, let down your hair!' she giggled. 'You really *are* pretty, Magda,' she decided rather wistfully. 'No wonder people fall for you.'

'Do they?' asked Magda, wryly. 'I like the way you use the plural. Thanks,' as she took the coffee.

Fran was sitting on the bed swinging her long legs.

'Yes,' she said, looking away, 'was I glad to hear you'd taken up with that nice Doctor Gregory. And I do mean that in the sense that you're good friends, only, at least up to now. It makes what I have to tell you a bit easier, you being fancy-free and all that.'

'What *have* you got to tell me, Fran?' Magda asked quietly. 'Ever since we met you've been like a hen with a dozen chicks running round her, pecking here and pecking there and never at ease. So out with it. I'm listening.'

NINETEEN

Fran stood up and regarded a ladder in her tights. 'There goes another fifty pence,' she decided. 'It's about the wedding, really. Saturday's wedding. You know?'

'Of course I know,' Magda tried not to imagine her heart had taken a dip. 'I don't suppose it was called off at the last moment?' she asked, trying to make it sound like a joke, 'or that anybody got cold feet and didn't turn up? One Winnie

265

Twine in a hospital is quite enough.'

'Oh, no, nothing like that. Twine's going ahead again, by the way, at Whitsun. We're all invited. No, there was a wedding all right. Elsie Lyons was invited to the reception, as you know.'

'They had a lovely day for it,' Magda commented, 'not like today.'

'That's true. No, it was a quiet, dignified wedding and Sister was honestly amazed that so much had got out. It now appears it was so much but not enough.'

'Whatever do you mean?' Magda asked.

'Well, we'd boobed. At least—Elsie Lyons had. You know how she was always Sister Fulham's great champion? Well, when she was invited at the last moment to drink the happy couple's health she discovered her boob.'

'And that was—?' Magda prompted, as Fran looked like drying up.

'That Sister had married Doctor O'Connor, a local G.P. She's now Mrs. O'Connor.

Magda had gone very pale and Fran's voice became anxious.

'I want to apologise, Magda, for all of us, for interfering the way we did in your affairs. We feel very foolish. We tried to find you last night but—of course—you were in Brighton. It didn't really make any difference to your love-life, did it? I mean Meg did say you had told her Doctor Devon was an old friend of yours, old in the sense of being *passé*. We didn't break anything up, did we? God! I hope not. When I heard you'd gone off with Nat Gregory I thought "Good! Two of the nicest people in the hospital together at last."'

'How did Jon come into all this?' Magda asked in a dead sort of voice. 'I hope Sister Fulham didn't lead him on a wild goose chase and then drop him for this O'Connor?'

'No, no,' Fran said impatiently. 'It never was Doctor Devon in that quarter. There's an explanation of how they came to appear so close, spend so much time together. If I tell you Sister's deceased *fiancé* was called Martin Devon, and died last year in a car crash, would you begin to see? He was Jon Devon's cousin. When those two spent such a lot of time together he was comforting and consoling her. One had lost a sweetheart and the other a relative and a friend. I believe Jon and Martin trained together and they were real pals.'

'I have met Martin,' Magda said. 'I

didn't hear he'd been killed.'

'When we warned you off the grass, regarding Doctor Devon, it was an intolerable interference. Then sending you to Coventry—! If one could go back in time and rub out one's mistakes, how much easier it would be! Tell me we haven't done any irreparable harm, Magda. We don't know how much you really liked Jon Devon, or he, you. But we felt so guilty you wouldn't believe—!'

'I saw him with my own eyes,' Magda spoke like one in a trance, 'dressed up to the nines with a carnation in his buttonhole. I even wished him luck and he said, "Thanks, I'll need it."'

'Well, he was best man, wasn't he?' Fran demanded. 'He must have had a lot on his mind with the organization and the speeches and—and everything.'

'And the thought of his new job coming up,' Magda mused.

'Oh, I didn't know that.'

'Well, forget it, then!' Magda shouted. 'For once keep your mouth shut about something which doesn't concern you!'

Fran looked as though she was going to cry.

'I'm sorry,' Magda said. 'Would you go,

now, Fran, please?'

'Aren't you going to break something over my head?'

'What good would that serve?' Magda asked.

'Well, I know it would do me a lot of good if I was in your shoes. You've taken it very well, I must say. Elsie will be relieved you're so calm about it. I'll go, then. If—if you want to talk to Doctor Devon I know he's about somewhere. I heard him being paged and he passed me like a flash going towards Victoria. Now I really *am* going.'

'Calm?' thought Magda as the door closed on her friend. 'Am I calm? I've just heard Jon's still free and that I've been breaking my heart for nothing and I still look calm? I feel as calm as a volcano must just before it erupts. There's no reason why Jon should look at me again, the way I've been with him, lately, snapping and being insolent like a petulant deb. He didn't know what I—and others—mistakenly thought. How could he? But I, for one, should have known how expert these places are at turning fiction into fact. I must write him while he is still here; write him at once and have it delivered to his room. Otherwise he will leave the hospital thinking I'm just a brat he found out in time.'

She eagerly put pen to paper at the dressing table and tore up page after page. The wording had to be just right. It was the most difficult letter of her life to compose, but she finally finished it.

'Dear Jon,' she wrote finally,

'I know that you will soon be leaving Darfield Park for your new appointment, and, knowing you, I'm sure that you intend to slip away without saying goodbye to anybody, which is why I have to write this letter while I still know where to find you.

Since we met up again in this hospital you have always favoured me with your friendship and, later, with a warmer regard which I eventually told you I was not prepared to return. Unfortunately for me I did return it, but I was given to understand by that sturdy growth, the grapevine, that there was an existing relationship between you and Sister Fulham, of which the hospital seemed to approve and upon which, I gathered, it would be unkind to intrude.

To put matters in a nutshell I thought you were marrying Jane on Saturday, and nothing that was said dissuaded me from so doing. I was really amazed and in a state of shock when I returned from weekend leave to learn from a colleague how wrong we had all been. I have been rude and brusque to you in past weeks to hide my true feelings. These are that I will be truly sorry to see you go for personal reasons, but proud and glad for you, also, that success and recognition appear to be crowning your career. I want you to know I wish you well and hope you will be very happy.

You are not to allow this letter to influence your actions, or plans, in any way, as a lot of water has passed under the bridge since we were sweethearts. I merely wish you to believe that there have been many misunderstandings and hope my explanations have cleared the air a little.

It has been most stimulating working under you.

> Yours very sincerely,
> Magda Warren.'

She read it twice and decided there was no more time for revising it. At the entrance to the doctors' residential wing she caught the eye of a woman in a sari.

'Doctor Bannerji—'

'My dear—?'

'Would you—could you see Doctor Devon gets this letter, please? You don't know me, but I'm his Staff-nurse on Victoria Ward. It's information he ought to have before tomorrow.'

'Very well, Staff-nurse,' Doctor Bannerji looked rather old-fashioned, as though she delivered illicit mail regularly. 'I'll take the letter to him if you like, but as he's in his room, why don't you—?'

'Oh, I wouldn't dare!' Magda was glad of the rule which forbade the nursing staff the doctors' wing. 'It isn't done, is it, Doctor? Thanks again.'

She didn't sleep much that night and yet, when she did, was conscious of waking minus a heavy load in her chest. First thing in the morning she remembered to ask the Senior Medical Officer for news of Doctor Gregory.

'Oh, he'll live,' she was told. 'An officer in the barracks is driving him home. He should be with us again by tomorrow.'

'Thank you, sir.'

It was a still, warm, misty morning and there was nothing about it to tell Magda Warren that it was to prove her last day as Staff-nurse on Victoria Ward at Darfield Park Hospital; nothing to inform her that when the new Medical Wing was opened to the public she would not be there to see the opening ceremony performed by the royal duchess, and parade in the new sky-blue overall, with white collar and cuffs, which was already on the drawing-board of a fashion artist for those of her rank to brighten the new, modern environs.

Outside the hum of the traffic was heavy and intrusive; if one opened the ward windows for air the noise came in. Being a bank holiday there was a great exodus from Darfield Park and the whole East End for the pleasures of country and coast. Hospitals however worked as usual, and this holiday Darfield Park was relieving St. Nicholas', and the ululations of the ambulances were much in evidence from the earliest hours.

During breakfast Nurse Twine had said, as Magda arrived at the table they shared in the dining-room, 'I feel in my bones that this is going to be one hell of a day.'

'You and your bones, Twine!' sneered Anne Gideon. 'They've been promising doomsday ever since I've known you.'

There was some sheepish avoidance of

glances as Magda had seated herself.

'Fran's told you,' Meg said, uncomfortably, 'but may I say we're most awfully sorry we interfered.'

'What's this,' asked Winnie.

'Oh, you, shut up!' Fran snapped. 'It's nothing to do with you.'

'No harm done, I'm sure,' Magda said quickly, before there could be any row. 'What about you, Meg? I believe you had a bit of a fright?'

'You can say that again. I'm to see the Fuehrer later, but it hasn't happened since, and I won't complain if it doesn't happen again.'

'What? What?' Winnie insisted. 'Have I been missing something?'

Meg picked up the daily paper from the floor, a small oblong pencilled in, and handed it to Magda. 'Did you know about this?'

Magda read a small item tucked away into a corner which gave the news that Divina Carlyon, retired actress of stage and television, had died in her sleep the previous morning.

'Oh, no!' she exclaimed, and felt sad. She only hoped that nothing her daughter Debbie had done had helped to bring on the fatal collapse. There was something gone out of her own life with Divina's passing, as she and her activities had served as the background to Magda's initiation as Staff-nurse on Victoria Ward, now seeming so very long ago, and so filled with event, as is any new experience.

One could not stay long repining, however, and now she was on her ward realizing they were a valuable nurse short. Clements was having a day off duty. She chivvied the younger girls, herself, leaving Nurse Augustine to interpret the night report. Soon there would be another staff changeover, just when she had licked this lot into shape.

Sister came on duty picking on everybody. Why wasn't Staff-nurse in the office? When she wanted junior nurses to read reports *she* would give the order. Why weren't breakfasts off the ward? Why wasn't the bed-pan round started?'

'Sister?' Magda breathlessly relieved poor Nurse Augustine from the tirade. 'I'm sorry, but I thought I ought to supervise breakfasts seeing Nurse Clements is off duty. I asked Nurse to read the report. She's got to learn sometime.'

'Isn't that for me to say, Staff-nurse?'

'Oh, dear!' thought Magda. 'Her corn must be bad again.'

'I'm sorry, Sister,' she said, aloud. 'It won't happen again'

'I should think not indeed. Now please do get on!'

Magda sensed rather than saw Jon Devon, and proceeded to roll up the cuff of the sphygnomanometer she had been using.

'Sister says you'll take me round, Staff-nurse.'

There was nothing in his request to imply that he had read her letter, but she knew that he would not refer to such a personal matter on duty.

'Certainly, Doctor,' she said dutifully.

Between the second and third beds she thought he was going to weaken but all he said was, 'Have you heard about —Divina?'

'Er—yes. Sad, isn't it? I suppose it was always a possibility.'

'I will be sending some flowers. Would you like your name to be included on the card?'

'Oh, I would. Thanks for—suggesting it. I always told her she was very special. My first patient.'

She wondered when he would refer to her letter, how it had affected him and if he would react in any way. He might simply say, 'Thanks for your letter,' and leave her guessing. What more should she be expecting after all this time? The flames fanned by the Founder's Day Dance had died out long ago; a few grey ashes probably stirred in his remembrance, if anything, after all this time.

In the middle of the drinks round Sister called, 'Staff-nurse! We've got an emergency coming up. A woman collapsed in Casualty and they're having difficulty finding a pulse. We'll be giving her oxygen, so number two bed. Got that? I've paged Doctor Devon.'

Winnie Twine arrived with the stretcher trolley holding a portable oxygen container with the mask over the patient's face. She proceeded to help transfer the woman into the warmed bed and Magda plugged the mask into the permanent oxygen supply by the bedhead.

'Thanks,' said Magda. 'Not busy in your department, then?'

'It's crowded,' said Winnie, 'but I've just had an awful shock and Sister told me to go away and relax for five minutes. They brought George in. He's been shot.'

Magda was using a stethoscope on the patient and thought she hadn't heard right.

'George—shot?' she echoed.

'That's right. He was passing the bank when he became suspicious about a fellow apparently keeping watch outside. He accosted this chap and next thing there was all this blasting away and George fell down, a bobby, too. The gang had been busy all weekend, apparently, and made off with three hundred-thousand quid.'

'And how is George?'

'They won't tell me. The bobby got hit in the leg, but from what I saw of George he caught it in the chest.'

Sister appeared and said, 'Staff-nurse?' looking coldly at Winnie. 'What are you doing here?'

Magda said hastily, 'Nurse Twine's fiancé has been brought in shot, Sister, and Sister Casualty has told Nurse Twine to take a bit of time off. She's upset.'

'Oh, dear! dear!' said Sister. 'Well, you take your oxygen equipment back to Casualty, Staff-nurse, where they might need it, and then come back and we'll have a little talk in my office. There's a good girl. Just now we must get on.'

Winnie trailed off looking somehow lost. Magda felt more sorry for one who had always been the outsider in their group than at any time in their acquaintance, and was sad she couldn't do anything about her, personally.

'How's our patient?' Sister Golightly asked, borrowing the stethoscope from Magda. 'Sounds pretty good to me. She's had coramine, of course?'

'According to her notes, Sister, yes.'

'Shot?' Sister seemed suddenly to realize what had been told her. 'Here in Darfield Park?'

'Yes. All over the holiday weekend a gang have apparently been at work and poor George, who was on his way here, no doubt, to see Winnie—that is, Staff-nurse Twine—became suspicious and came in for their unwelcome attentions.'

'I'll be especially kind to that girl when she comes back. Meanwhile we seem to have lost Dr. Devon, temporarily, but Doctor Patel's coming along. I'll just go and take Mrs. Rouse's dialysis reading. You stay here 'til somebody comes.'

Doctor Patel arrived, urbane, black-haired, a really handsome Asian. He examined the patient and after a few moments decided, 'Look, Staff, she's ticking over very nicely and I'm not going to disturb her further until we can get her E.C.Gd. Can you get somebody to sit with her? Somebody sensible?'

'I'll just get Nurse Augustine, Doctor. Sister sent her to the Path. Lab. but she should be back. I'll have a look.'

So it was that Magda was passing the broom-cupboard when the blast from an explosion blew it towards her and behind it was a solid sheet of bluish, yellowish flame and a dull roar. Magda felt the solid blow of the blast and noted a crumpled blue figure on the floor of the broom cupboard. She dived in without more ado and dragged, wondering, foolishly, if she had got her priorities right. Should she have gone for the casualty or the fire bell first? She heard the din of the bell's summons as she doused the last of the flames on the victim with her bare hands, so obviously someone had pressed the red button. She looked down at the twisted features of Winnie Twine, her spectacles cracked with heat still on her face and part of her dress burnt into charcoal.

'Oh, God!' said Magda, feeling suddenly very odd. 'Oh, God!' she had tried to

280

remove Winnie's glasses but, instead, a piece of skin from her own hand remained attached to them. She was aware of figures with fire-extinguishers and buckets and then one face stood out among the rest.

'Magda! you stupid, heroic little fool!' said Jon Devon, emotionally, and then she fainted.

TWENTY

They said they had told her many times how the whole thing had happened, but it was three days before Magda at last absorbed the facts as they were presented to her by Sister Golightly.

'It seems, Staff-nurse, that our visitor from Casualty didn't feel like going back to her department immediately, and shut herself in our broom-cupboard for a quiet smoke and a think. She doesn't smoke, normally, but it had become a nervous habit with her of late. She had the portable oxygen equipment with her, of course, and while she was fumbling around in there had accidentally turned the tap on. Well, you can imagine the rest. A struck match and whoomph! She was lucky to get out of there alive, thanks to you, and though she has a few second degree burns on her legs she's going to be all right in time.'

'And George?'

'The fiancé? They took a bullet out of his shoulder. It had missed his lung by a hair's breadth. He's walking about being a nuisance, actually. How're the hands?'

'Oh, much less painful now, Sister.'

'You did very well, you know. I'm proud of you.'

'Oh, Sister! Anyone would have—'

'We don't know that, do we? In theory we're probably all heroes and heroines, but in the event how many would actually sail in and just do what had to be done? You're not going to get out of a commendation, so stop trying.'

'Who's doing my job?'

'A girl who's just finished a night stint, called Faraday. She might do. I have hopes of her eventually.'

'But what about me eventually? When I'm better?'

Sister gave an odd little laugh.

'That's been taken out of my hands, Staff-nurse. Anyhow, you stay put and get better. Just look at all these flowers. You must have a lot of wealthy friends. Red roses in April? Good gracious me!'

Meg came next. 'How're things, Magda?'

'I'm fine. I feel a fraud lying here. I seem to have lost my job, according to Sister Golightly, and I was feeling a bit depressed until you came in.'

'Everybody wants to see you. The S.N.O. vets all your visitors. I represent our lot, by the way, they all wanted to come but I drew the short straw.'

'I should be asking how you are, Meg.'

'Faintly disorganized but by no means down and out. I'm told I have very mild symptoms and that they could disappear in time. On a wave of euphoria I went out with one of your boy friends. I hope you don't mind? He's nice.'

'Oh?' Magda smiled faintly, and something hurt inside where she had not been burnt. 'Have a good time?'

'Very. We're repeating the experiment at the weekend. Yes, indeed, I find Nat Gregory very charming.'

Magda said quickly, 'He's O.K. again, then?'

'From Montezuma's revenge, you mean?' Meg laughed. 'Oh, yes. Well, mustn't stay any longer.' She stooped and kissed the other. 'Well done! We're all enormously proud to know you.'

She was told by a nurse whose name she didn't know to sleep for the next hour, and dutifully allowed herself to be eased down on her pillows. But she couldn't sleep. 'Why hasn't he been?' she fretted. 'Did he get my letter? Has he gone? But he wouldn't. He—'

'Doctor, no! She's resting. I tell you—'

But the door burst open and there was Jon, with, briefly, the same look he had had on his face when he had swept her into his arms as she had lost her senses. This was swiftly controlled, however.

'Well?' he demanded. 'How are we?'

She didn't know but the joy of seeing him had made her look lovely. She wore a white nightdress with pink rose-buds appliqued over it and was any normal young woman apart from her white-swathed hands carefully strapped to rests so that she couldn't knock them. She knew, now, that when she had opened her eyes on occasion, after the accident, Jon's face had always swum into her sight before she slid away, again, and now she noticed there were great hollows under his eyes as though he hadn't slept for nights.

'You got my letter?' she asked politely.

'What letter? *What letter?*'

'Oh, no! I gave Doctor Bannerji a letter to give to you the night before the accident.'

'That woman? She's so nosey she would read it and then drop it down the nearest loo. Anyway, what did it say?'

'I can't remember every word. It took me hours to write. I think—in a nutshell—it conveyed the fact that I love you.'

He sat down on the bed and looked for something to hold, but desisted.

'Don't say that unless you mean it, for I never stopped loving you, Magda. I told you about my efforts to forget you. They weren't too successful.'

'I mean it, Jon. I mean it now and forever. I've discovered that if you aren't honest with yourself you can never find happiness.'

'Oh,' he reached out his arms and asked, 'Where don't you hurt?'

'I didn't burn my lips, Jon. You can try them out if you want to.'

He kissed her gently and yet she knew that when the time was right for such things his lips would stir the power of

Niagara between them.

'Oh, Magda!' his laugh was almost a sob. 'Your parents have been in and out but you've just slept and slept. I tried to tell them that shock affected some people that way, and I also told them I was going to ask you to marry me the minute you were conscious. I've been in a sort of state of shock myself, saying all sorts of wild things.'

'It's all right by me, Jon,' she told him. 'I'm willing.'

'I've been an awful nuisance, too. The Burns Unit people hate my guts. I have to fight an awful woman even to get near you.'

He kissed her again, still gently, but more lingeringly, so that deep within her nerves began to shrill.

When Sister opened the door with her hip this was how she saw them, and she without even one hand to defend herself, the poor, wee lamb!

Sister decided to slide out again, as she had apparently been unobserved, and muttering under her breath went down the corridor complaining, as generations of nurses before her, that at this rate she would never get done in time.

This Large Print Book for the Partially sighted, who cannot read normal print, is published under the auspices of

THE ULVERSCROFT FOUNDATION